Constant

Venorique Braies

Contents

Chapter 1

(PETER)

Jericho had been the first to notice the two women making their way through the field of boulders. He had motioned to Peter and Ellie to catch their attention. The three of them watched the zig-zag motion that the two women ran in as they tried to stay out of sight. Ellie motioned with her chin out farther in the darkness behind the two women. There was a man following closely behind them. Ellie glared at the man and reached back for her bow that was always hanging on her shoulder. Peter nodded at her. The three of them had been tracking the large group that was camped out in the field in front of them.

They had followed the progress of the group and they had seen the two women in chains. There had been a plan to rescue the women but the right time hadn't presented itself. Now that the women were running straight to them it seemed like the right time to step in. The man who had been behind the two women managed to loop around and sprint in front of them. He was now blocking their path to the safety of the trees.

"Where do you think you're going?" He asked and one of the women lunged forward at him.

Ellie released the arrow and it drove into the man's back. The two women who he had been blocking from entering the cover of the trees stepped back in shock.

"Nice shot," Peter whispered and he saw her smile. One of the women gasped as she saw the man fall to the ground in front of her. Her hand flew up to her mouth and she stood motionless for a few seconds. The other woman started scanning the trees with her eyes to figure out where the arrow had come from and if the shooter was a friend or foe. She glanced back behind her shoulder reached for the hand of her companion. She pulled her friend behind her and the two women raced froward.

Jericho, Peter, and Ellie dropped down from the branches that they had been perched on and hurried to the edge of the trees. Jericho moved behind one of the women and Peter moved behind the other. Peter was close enough to see her blonde hair in the moonlight. The blonde girl gasped when she looked at her companion and saw Jericho's large frame behind her friend. Before she could make another sound Peter stepped up and grabbed her around the waist and covered her mouth. She squirmed in his arms in an attempt to get away from him. This just made Peter hold her tighter against him. When she made to stomp on his foot and bite his hand Peter scooped her up in his arms and walked into the trees.

Once they were deeper into the trees Peter set her down on her own two feet but he didn't let go of her. She was still held tightly against him and struggling more than ever. He trapped her arms down at her sides hoping that she would be easier to manage. Peter didn't notice the dagger in her hand until she attempted to drive it backwards into his thigh.

"Hey!" Peter hissed in her ear as he realized what she was trying to do. "We're trying to help you!" She went completely still in his arms and stopped struggling. Peter looked up at Jericho in shock. Jericho shrugged. The girl that he was holding wasn't even putting up a fight. She just looked frightened. "Do you promise to be nice?" He asked and she nodded her reply. Peter was hesitant to uncover her mouth but he figured she wouldn't scream. What he didn't figure on was that she would turn around and shove him away with all of her might. Peter stumbled backwards as she marched towards Jericho with her dagger raised out in front of her.

"Let her go!" She hissed.

"Now there's no reason for all of that," Ellie interjected and Peter nearly sighed in relief as the blonde girl turned to stare at her with an open mouth. She hadn't expected a woman to be out in the trees. She walked forward towards the dagger wielding woman and Peter took a step forward to jump in the middle if he needed to protect her. "My name is Ellie, what's yours?" She asked casually.

"Ryah," The blonde girl whispered.

"It is a pleasure to make your acquaintance Ryah," Ellie said offering the girl a hand. Ryah looked down at the dagger in her hand and slipped it into the pocket of her dress. Peter wondered what other things she had hidden in that pocket of hers. She extended her hand and took Ellie's giving it a slight shake. "What about you?" Ellie asked looking in the direction of the girl that Jericho was holding. "Jericho, you can let her go now," she said politely and he immediately let her go.

"Anna," said a timid voice.

"It is wonderful to meet the two of you," Ellie said. "Now, we need to run."

Ellie turned and took off in the direction of their horses. Ryah and Anna looked at each other in confusion. Jericho took Anna's hand in his and led her in the dark. Peter reached for Ryah's hand and she jerked her arm away from him.

"I am perfectly capable of running on my own," She spat then took off following Jericho and the rest of the group. Peter laughed silently then followed after her. In just a few seconds she stumbled over a large root and fell on the ground.

"Are you now?" Peter whispered under his breath. He could tell from the way that she pushed herself back up to her feet that she was exhausted. He offered her a hand when she was back on her feet and to his surprise she accepted his offering.

They reached the horses within a few minutes of running and Peter released her hand only to grab her around the waist and throw her up onto the horse. He managed to sit in the saddle in front of her. When the horse took off at a trot she grabbed his hips to keep from falling off of the horse. Immediately she released her hold.

"You've been through a lot," He said over his shoulder to her after a few minutes of silence. She didn't reply so he searched his mind to find something else to say to her that might encourage her to speak up.

"So, you're Ryah, that's a pretty name. My name is Peter, while it isn't a particularly pretty name it is prestigious," He straightened in the saddle for emphasis. "My parents must have known that I was going to grown up and be a prestigious man."

"Either that or they knew you would need something to live up to," She said and Peter laughed at her quick humor.

"She has jokes!" He said, "So, where are you from?"

"Anna and I were abducted during a raid. We will be rescued," she said with so much confidence that Peter actually believed her.

"We would be happy to take you home but we don't have any boats. We don't live close enough to any of the harbors to have boats. But, I am sure that we could talk to someone who we have a treaty with."

"We would appreciate that," she said and Peter looked back to grin over his shoulder at her. They continued riding throughout the day. The sun had risen to show the state of the women. They were filthy and he could tell that they were exhausted. Neither of them had had a decent meal or sleep in days. Peter reached into a pocket of his saddle to pass Ryah some of the dried meat that he had carried on him. It was supposed to be his lunch but he didn't mind sharing with her. She needed it more than he did. Once the meat disappeared he dug down and found an apple that he had been saving. He smiled as she used the knife to slice the fruit in half and she reached over to hand Anna a piece. Everything that Ryah had she shared with her traveling companion. Ryah made sure that Anna had something to eat before she ate anything herself. Peter noticed how she gave Anna the better half of the apple and kept the slightly bruised half for herself.

It was beginning to get dark when they finally stopped for the day. Peter swung off of the horse and reached up for Ryah. To his surprise she leaned forward and allowed him to put his hands on her waist to help lift her down onto her feet. When he placed her on the ground she started shaking out her legs. It had been a few hours since their last break. Typically they didn't make the horses go so far in a day but they were trying to put as much distance between themselves and the group that had been in the field.

Peter loosened the saddle on his horse and led him over to the stream that was running nearby. The animal leaned its large head down and started drinking. Peter rubbed its neck as it quenched its thirst.

"Peter!" Ryah called and he spun around to see her with her arms around Anna keeping her upright. He rushed over to them.

"What's wrong?!" He asked as he wrapped an arm around Anna to help support her.

"I think that she is sick," Ryah replied and Peter looked over at Ellie. She hurried over to look at Anna.

"We will find you somewhere to rest for awhile," Ellie said turning back to her horse and tightening the saddle again. Peter realized what she was talking about. The only place that was nearby enough to consider was Roderick's castle.

"Ellie..." Peter whispered as he thought of all of the things that had happened at the castle. She clearly thought that something was wrong with Anna or she wouldn't have suggested it in the first place. He knew that the castle was full of terrible memories. Memories that still haunted her dreams all of these years later.

"It'll be fine," She replied in a happy tone. "It's just a few minutes away, we will have to get back on the horses. Peter waited for Jericho to get his horse ready and Jericho swung up into the saddle. He waited and Peter lifted Anna up to sit in front of Jericho so he could help support her. Peter tightened his own saddle and swung up onto his horse. He reached down to offer Ryah a hand which she accepted and he swung her up on the saddle behind him.

"Where are we going?" Ryah whispered.

"Somewhere safe," Peter replied. "We are going to a castle." Peter felt Ryah sit up taller and lean slightly forward. He could feel the warmth from her closeness radiating through his shirt onto his back.

"Who lives there?" She asked and her breath tickled his neck.

"Just ghosts from the past," he replied trying to ignore her closeness.

"Ghosts?" She asked in confusion.

"Lots of them," Peter replied and that seemed to satisfy her because she leaned back and didn't ask anymore questions. They reached the castle and Ellie went inside through the secret entrance.

"Come with me," Ellie said when she returned from inside the castle. Peter stepped forward to help pry a larger hole that would be big enough to allow Anna and Ryah to get inside. Peter stepped back out into the night allowing Ellie to take Ryah and Anna deeper into the castle. A few minutes later Ellie came back out.

"Where did you take them?"

"To the dining room I lit them a fire."

"Once I see to the horses I will take up some wood."

Jericho pulled open the door to the stables and they were met with the dusty smell of a barn. Jericho managed to light a torch and place it on the wall to offer them some light as they settled the horses in for the night. The three of them worked to get a space cleared for the animals then offered them some feed after they had their saddles off. Jericho said that he would see to the animals if Peter wanted to go get wood for the fire. Peter nodded and set off into the trees. He managed to find several pieces of wood that would be perfect for the fire. He slipped back inside the entrance and made his way through the dark from memory.

He went up the stairs and rounded the corners. Up ahead he could see the light glowing from the small fire that Ellie had made to chase away the darkness while the women waited. He looked in the dining room to see Ryah walking around the room looking at the portraits on the wall.

"Terrifying isn't it?" Peter asked and she jumped as the sound echoed around the room. He took a few of his sticks over to the fireplace and put them on the flame that was starting to dwindle.

"I thought it was rather beautiful," Ryah said as she continued to walk around the room.

"This place is full of horrors," Peter said feeling his stomach churn at her sense of awe. She turned around to look at him waiting for him to continue.

"This place was ruled by a man named Roderick, he was the epitome of evil." Peter felt bile raise up in the back of his throat as he thought about Roderick and all of the horrible things that he had done. Ryah was waiting for more of an explanation but she wasn't going to get one. Peter brushed his hands off of his trousers then dropped the wood against the wall near the door. "I need to tend to the horses," He said and rushed out of the room. Peter walked out the door and leaned against the wall. Ellie made him jump as she rounded the corner with her arms full of firewood that would see them through the night. He offered to take the wood from her so she could see to Ryah and Anna. She gave him a confused look but didn't question him as she walked into the room.

"Those were from the ropes," Her feminine voice rang out through the darkness over the popping of the fire. Peter squeezed his eyes shut as he imagined what Ryah was looking at.

"Ropes?" Ryah asked softly.

Peter tried to stop his mind as he thought of all of the terrible things that had happened to Ellie at the hands of Roderick. She didn't seem bothered as she went through the details with Ryah giving her a small explanation of the horrors that she had endured. Peter tried to think of something else, anything else, to get the images out of his mind.

There was a hand on his shoulder and he nearly dropped the wood that was in his arms.

"Are you alright?" Jericho asked. Peter nodded and the two men walked into the dining room.

"Should we find somewhere to sleep for the night?" Ellie asked. She found the wood that Peter had left near the door and she scooped it up in her arms as Ryah supported Anna into the room that Ellie led them to. Ellie placed her wood next to the fireplace and helped Anna into the large bed that dominated the room. Peter and Jericho started to coax a fire to a blaze. Ellie gave Anna her bed roll and made sure that Anna laid down. Ryah was standing next to Anna holding her hand with a nervous look on her face. Soon there was a roaring fire in the fireplace and Ryah released Anna's hand. She walked over to the fireplace and sat down in front of it. She laid down on her side and Peter pulled his bedroll out of his pack. He rolled it out and held it open for Ryah. She looked at him with a shocked expression on her face.

"I can't take this," She said stubbornly. She didn't know that Peter was equally as stubborn as she was.

"You can and you will, now climb in and go to sleep." He dropped the bedroll and walked out the door. Peter looked at Jericho who was sitting on his bedroll. He scooted over to make room for Peter to sit down as well. Peter was grateful to at least have a soft spot to sit for the night as they kept watch.

Chapter 2

(PETER)

Peter was just beginning to nod off after Jericho had just taken over for his shift of the watch. His head dropped down on his chest and Jericho reached down to tap Peter's knee making him jerk awake. He blinked sleepily at Jericho knowing that there was no way that it was time for his watch again. Jericho motioned down the hallway. There was a sound down the hall and Peter jumped up with Jericho at his side. They grabbed the bedroll and hauled it into the room and closed the door behind them. The fire had died down to just a few glowing embers. Peter could see Ryah's outline in front of the fireplace. Peter went over to Ellie and placed a hand on her shoulder. Her eyes opened and she emerged from her cloak that she had wrapped around herself to keep warm.

"What is it?" She whispered.

"Someone is here," Peter whispered in reply.

She went over to Anna to wake her up. Ellie held a finger at her lips indicating that Anna should be quiet. Anna didn't make a peep as Ellie walked over to Ryah to wake her up as well. Ellie motioned for Ryah to go over by Anna. When she obeyed Ellie went for her bow and crouched by the fire waiting for whoever was coming up the stairs. There was a glow of a torch out in the hall that could be seen underneath the door. Jericho went and stood next to the door and Peter moved over to stand next to the bed in front of Anna and Ryah. They were ready for whoever was coming through the door.

The door swung open and a figure stepped into the room. Jericho was lifting his sword to cut down the man when Ellie yelled "Down!" Immediately their weapons hit the floor. Peter watched as Ellie ran forward and launched herself into the arms of the man in the doorway.

"Ellie?" Peter heard Ben ask as his arms wrapped around her holding her close.

"What are you doing here?" Ellie asked.

"What are you doing here?" Ben replied.

"You could have gotten yourself killed," Peter said as he leaned down to pick up his sword.

"You couldn't shoot me if you tried." Ben replied and Peter reached for the bow that Ellie had dropped and drew back an arrow.

"Peter," Ellie warned and Peter lowered the bow with a frown on his face.

"What are you doing here Ben?" Peter asked.

"I saw the light from your fire and I came to kick out whoever was inside the castle. I noticed your horses down below. What about you?"

Ellie motioned over to Ryah and Anna. "We found them at the edge of the forest and we needed a place to stay for the night."

"Of all places, this is where you decided to stay?" Ben said his voice rising slightly with each word. "You shouldn't even be traveling... "He started to say and Ellie pressed her lips against his cutting him off. "This isn't over," He said sternly when she pulled away from him.

"Are you pregnant again?" Peter asked as he imagined the other four children at home.

"Maybe," She replied playfully.

"Congratulations!" Peter said and hurried over to wrap both Ben and Ellie in a large hug. "If it is a girl will you please consider Peterina as an appropriate name? Or Petera? I could come up with something else if you would prefer."

"Will you let go of that awful name already? We already have little Petey," Ellie said as she shoved his shoulder away. Peter laughed as he held his hands up in a surrender.

"Just consider it, that's all I'm asking."

"We are being rude," Ellie said looking back at Ben. "I didn't even introduce our traveling companions."

Everyone turned to look towards Ryah and Anna. Ben followed their gazes ans looked towards the two women standing next to the bed.

"This is my husband Benjamin," Ellie said. "This is Anna and Ryah. They were abducted from their home and we will hopefully be able to help them on their journey home."

"It's nice to meet the two of you," Ben said. "When were you planning on heading out?" He asked.

"Are you feeling any better?" Ellie asked Anna as she took her hand.

"Much better," Anna replied even though she didn't look like she felt much better. She was still dirty and looked just as tired as before. "Thank you."

"Do you think that you could travel?" Ellie asked and Anna nodded.

"Once we get something to eat and see to the horses we should be able to start moving towards Cheddix."

Ellie helped Ryah and Anna take care of their bed rolls as Jericho, Peter, and Ben went out to see to the horses. As the men led the horses out of the stables Ellie helped Ryah get Anna out of the castle. Ryah emerged squinting in the light of morning. Peter swung up on his horse and offered her a hand up. They started off and all that Peter could think of was Ellie's announcement that she was pregnant again. All of their other children held a special place in his heart.

He talked about the twins and how wonderful they were. He talked about brave little Petey and how he was learning so many things. He then started talking about Thea.

"Is she your girlfriend?" Ryah asked.

"The prettiest girl I have ever seen!" Peter replied enthusiastically.

"Get your eyes off of my seven year old daughter or I will shoot you myself," Ellie said as she trotted by on her horse without bothering to look at Peter.

"She's joking," Peter whispered to Ryah once Ellie was out of earshot.

"No, she's not!" Ellie yelled back to him letting him know that she had heard him.

Peter started talking about Ellie's other children. A little girl named Lilly who was six years old and the sweetest little girl. He then moved on to speak about the newest edition to the family. A little boy named Eric after

Ben's father. Ryah was quiet as Peter talked. She had been adding words of encouragement to keep him talking but now she was quiet.

"What's wrong?" Peter asked.

"Tell me about Eric," She requested, her voice thick with emotion.

"He's three and he is so smart. He has been running around and following his older siblings since before he turned one year old. He loves to climb up trees and chase the dog. he has curly brown hair and big blue eyes."

"You need to have a family of your own,"she said quietly as she noticed to how passionate he was talking about the children.

"I haven't found the right girl yet," he replied looking over his shoulder at Ryah. She was looking down at the ground. She was clearly troubled over something that he had said and he knew it wasn't the harmless flirting.

"Tell me about Eric," He said and she stiffened. Peter knew that he had hit exactly what she was troubled over. She took a few minutes considering what she should say.

"He died," She finally answered. Peter patiently waited for her to continue talking. "He..." She said and her voice shook.

"You don't have to tell me about him," Peter said and he felt bad for pushing her to talk.

"No, I... uh, he," She cleared her throat and continued to search for the right words. "He went on a raid with Torin and he took an arrow for Torin. The men tried their best to save him but he passed away," she blurted out quickly.

'This Torin must be a special man,' thought Peter.

"Who's Torin?" He asked.

"He's a good man," She replied.

"I see," Peter said looking forward. This man Torin meant something to her.

"You see what? Are we there?" She asked leaning to look over his shoulder again. Peter could feel her warmth again and searched for something to say. They weren't very close to home. She hadn't understood what he had been talking about. Eventually the town came into view.

"Mother!" Yelled Thea and Peter looked over to see her racing down the grassy hill towards them. Ellie jumped off of her horse to meet her little daughter and caught her in her arms.

Peter watched the happy reunion of the family and he wished for one of his own. The twins went over what had happened in the few days that Ellie had been gone. At the mention of the cookies that Susan had baked Thea, Lilly and Eric pulled their father up the hill towards home.

Petey stayed behind and looked towards Peter as he slid out of the saddle. Peter turned around to help Ryah down to her feet. Peter looked over and saw that Jericho was helping Anna down as well.

Petey had the reins of Ben's horse in his hand and he was watching Peter and Ryah.

"Hello," Petey said and he bowed to Ryah. Peter had to cover his smile so he turned to fiddle with the saddle on his horse.

"Hello Petey," Ryah said sweetly as she gave him a curtsy that made him look down at the ground. Once he had the courage to look up he gave her a smile.

"My friends call me Pete," He said and Peter tried to hold in his laughter. He covered up with a cough.

"Since when?!" Peter interjected and Ryah's elbow connected with his ribs making him jerk away.

"I am pleased to make your acquaintance Pete, My name is Ryah."

"Welcome to Cheddix," Pete said.

Jericho reached over to take Ellie's reins from her and led the two horses towards the stables. Peter led his horse away as well with Petey following closely behind him. Peter turned to watch as Ellie and and Ryah helped Anna up the hill. Petey was chatting happily about all of the things that had happened since Peter had been away. Peter didn't have to offer much encouragement for the little boy to continue with his account of what had happened.

They got all four of the horses brushed down and gave them food and water. Petey decided that he wanted some of Susan's cookies for himself. Torin watched him run towards the house. Peter wanted to join him but he knew that after so long traveling he wouldn't be welcome in Susan's house without cleaning up a bit first. He walked in the direction of the river that was flowing nearby. The water was primarily snow melt from up in the mountain so the water was usually freezing. Peter walked up to the edge of the water and pulled off his boots. He took a deep breath and stepped into the river. He gasped at the cold and took a few seconds to catch his breath. He grit his teeth and plunged ahead into the water and dunked himself beneath the surface. He came up gasping and shook his head sending water flying in all directions from his wet hair. He would clean up properly later but for now this would be good enough for him. He scrubbed the dirt away as quickly as he could and got out of the water before he could start shivering.

He climbed up on a large boulder at the edge of the river and allowed the sun to dry his clothing. Once he was mostly dried off he headed back towards the village. He walked through the door and the first thing he saw was a stunning woman.

He couldn't believe the transformation that Ryah had gone through. She was no longer covered in dirt wearing a filthy dress. She had been cleaned up and her hair was brushed and braided down her back. She looked at him with large blue eyes.

"You look different," Peter said. "You look nothing like that filthy girl that I snagged in the forest."

She smiled back at him and her eyes sparkled. "And you look nothing like that handsome chivalrous gentleman who saved my life, where is Jericho anyway?"

Susan burst out laughing and stepped forward to wrap an arm around Ryah's elbow. Peter stood there dumbstruck as Susan led her away down the hall. Peter couldn't take his eyes off of her as she walked away from him down the hall. Just before she rounded the corner out of view she turned to give him a dazzling smile and then she was gone.

"Get a grip Peter," he whispered to himself. "You act as though you've never seen a pretty girl before."

"You know, talking out loud to yourself is the first sign of insanity," Ben said from behind him causing him to jump.

"What's the second sign?" Peter asked. "Staring after a girl that I know I can never have?"

"You're right, she is out of your league," Ben replied. He stepped forward to cuff Peter on the back of the head. "Come on, Susan has prepared a meal for us."

Chapter 3

(PETER)

"Now that's not very nice!" Peter said as he held up his arms to get the horse to turn the other way. It took off in the other direction running the length of the corral. Petey was perched on the edge of the fence. He rested his head in his hands as he watched the horse run. Peter could imagine what he was thinking as he watched the sun reflect off of its mane. Petey had always loved horses. Peter glanced up to see Ryah and Thea walking towards the horse corral. Peter lifted his arm towards them when they looked up at him.

Peter could hear them talking to Petey but he couldn't hear what they were saying. Petey said something that made Thea step forward and glare at her brother. She said something to him and he reached over to shove her shoulder. Thea stumbled backwards and Ryah grabbed her before she could fall inside the corral.

"Petey!" Peter said as Peter took a step forward to prevent a fight but Ryah intervened.

"Yes, sir?" Petey asked timidly knowing that he had been caught doing something wrong.

"Men don't shove girls," Peter said and Petey slumped down further under the force of his voice. Peter hadn't meant to make Petey shrink back in fear.

"Yes sir," Petey replied and Peter could hear his voice shake. Thea and Petey started talking back and forth to each other and Ryah rolled her eyes. She stepped in between them on the fence post. Ryah said something that made both twins nod. She kept her eyes on the horse as it ran around the corral but her mouth was moving as she spoke to the children. Petey and Thea had their eyes on her face and their mouths were hanging open in awe as she spoke to them. Peter tried to hide that he was watching.

Petey jumped down off of the fence. "I bet I can catch more frogs than you!" He said loudly and Thea jumped down to join him.

"No you can't!" She yelled then sprinted after him with her braids flopping against her back. Ryah tipped her head back and laughed at their retreat. Peter walked up behind her and leaned his arms against the wood. Ryah turned around and jumped.

"How do you do that?!" She gasped as she held onto the fence with a white knuckled grip.

"Move silently and gracefully like a butterfly?" He asked earning a laugh from Ryah. "You're really good with them," He said looking in the direction of the running twins.

"They're sweet," She replied and Peter laughed loudly.

"Now, the twins have been called many things, but I don't think that a complete stranger has ever called them sweet. Especially right after hearing them argue."

Ryah shrugged "I think they're sweet."

Peter laughed as he took two of the horses back into their stalls. "So, did you come here to watch me expertly tame this wild beast?" He asked gesturing to the horse that started running away from him. Ryah dropped down off of the edge of the fence as the horse ran in her direction.

"I actually came here to watch you fall on your backside."

"Well, you shouldn't have to wait very long to get your wish." He said as he walked over to horse and got her saddle tightened. He stroked her nose and tried to get her to calm down. "It's alright," He whispered to the horse. He managed to get one foot in the stirrup and swing one leg over the horse's back. Peter sat securely in the saddle and looked down at Ryah's awed face as she stood next to the corral fence. Peter smiled at her and the horse started bucking. He scrambled to hold onto the reins but was thrown quickly. He rolled underneath the fence before the horse could crush him.

"You were right, I didn't have to wait long at all!" Ryah said with an extended hand to him. Peter took her offered hand and allowed her to pull him to his feet. Her hand felt so small in his and he didn't want to let go of her. She took her hand back and Peter bent to pick up an apple from a bucket that was sitting near the stable. Pulling a knife from his weapons stash he sliced through the crisp fruit and offered a piece to the horse. She was happy to take the treat and Peter wiped his hands on his pants.

"Should we see if the twins have drowned each other yet?" He asked and her blue eyes grew wide.

"They wouldn't..." She whispered. Peter laughed at her expression as he slung his bow over his shoulder and started off in the direction of the pond. Ryah was quiet as they walked and Peter wanted to hear the sound of her laugh.

"Did you know that I once saved a distressing damsel from the clutches of a vile criminal?" He asked and she didn't reply to his question. "Yes, it is true, you are walking side by side with a hero. I stormed the castle and saved the pretty lady and her defenseless oaf of a husband from an evil man."

"I thought it was Ellie who saved Rollo from Roderick," She said wrinkling her eyebrows.

"You don't believe me?" He asked placing his hand against his chest in a wounded gesture.

"I believe that you are twisting the truth," She laughed and Peter was victorious. "That story gets grander and more dangerous with each time that you tell it!"

"That's because I am in it!" He said proudly.

"Have you had any luck in securing a boat for Anna and I to return home?" Ryah asked and Peter hated to answer her. He didn't want to get her a boat. He wanted her to stay.

"I have sent a messenger to one of our allies. The messenger left yesterday. You should have your answer in a few days," He said. Peter found her a messenger quickly because he knew that she wanted to return home. He didn't want her to leave but he wouldn't force her to stay or be the one who delayed her departure.

"Thank you," She said sincerely and he knew how much it meant to her to get home. She had mentioned a man named Torin and he wondered if Torin had anything to do with the reason that she wanted to go home so badly.

"You're welcome."

They were almost to the stream and they could hear the twins yelling and splashing in the water. "I'll race you!" Ryah said suddenly and took off running. She lifted her skirt up in her hand as she sprinted. Peter gave her a few seconds head start and watched her run. He decided that he had given her enough of a lead and he took of following her.

"Go Ryah!" Peter heard Thea yell. 'Traitor' he thought.

"Go Peter!" Petey yelled and Peter knew that Petey really wanted Ryah to win the race but he didn't want to be the same as his sister. If Thea had said 'Go Peter' then Petey would have said 'Go Ryah'.

Peter launched forward and flew past Ryah. With his few seconds lead he kicked off his boots and shirt, dropped his bow, and dove into the water. The water was freezing which caused him to shoot up out of the stream. He shook his head and sprayed the twins with cold water. Thea held up her hands and wrinkled her nose as she blocked her face from the spray. Peter looked towards the shore and he saw Ryah standing there panting as she looked at him and at the stream.

Peter held up his hand and motioned for her to get in. She shook her head back and forth and took a step backwards. When she didn't move to join them he took a step towards her. Her eyes widened as she immediately realized his intention.

"No," She said holding up a finger in the air like she was scolding a naughty child. Peter wasn't afraid of her. He knew that he could scoop her up in his arms and toss her into the stream. In fact, that was exactly what he was planning on doing. It was like she could read his mind because she lifted her foot and grabbed her boot to pull it off of her foot. She threw it to the side and the second boot joined the first a few seconds later. Once her shoes were off she stepped into the stream and inched down in the cold water. Thea swam over to show Ryah something. It could have been anything that she had found. Peter watched her bend over and fuss over the treasure.

She would make an excellent mother one day. It was clear that the children adored her. They were constantly seeking her approval and listening to the things that she had to say. Thea splashed away and Ryah continued to look at what Thea had given her. Peter threw his arm across the water and a wall of water went in Ryah's direction. She took a step back with a gasp and fell down on her backside into the stream. Peter heard Petey roar with laughter and Thea turned to glare at him. Her lips twitched as she tried to keep from smiling. Out of nowhere a large glob of mud smacked Peter squarely in the chest and splattered up over his face and neck. He reached up and wiped at the mud. Thea had a large smile on her face as she watched.

"Oh sure, you're not going to scold her!" He said as he watched the little girl giggle. Petey was still roaring with laughter. Peter looked over at Ryah who was trying to look as innocent as possible as she wrung the water out of her long blonde hair.

She was distracted. Perfect time to strike.

Peter slowly dropped down and grabbed a handful of mud off of the bottom of the stream. Then he stood and threw it in Ryah's direction. At the last second she ducked and the mud flew over her. Thea and Petey flew over to Ryah's side and started flinging mud balls.

"That's not fair!" He yelled as mud flew in his direction. "Truce!" He said holding his hands up in the air. The three attackers turned to look at each other. Thea nodded and Petey shrugged then eventually nodded in agreement.

"Truce," Ryah agreed and walked over to where Peter was waiting with an outstretched hand. Peter took her hand and yanked. She crashed against his bare chest. Peter wrapped his arm around her waist securing her against him. She looked up at him with a shocked expression on her face. Peter smiled at her as he brought his other arm around and lifted a large glob of mud towards her face. She pushed against his chest but she was no match for him. He smeared the mud over her smooth skin. Her forehead and cheeks were painted with long dark streaks. As a final touch he tapped the tip of her nose and released her. She reached up and unsuccessfully tried to wipe the mud away. He smiled at her and then walked away with his head held high in victory. Before he could get too far away Ryah crashed against him. He barely managed to get a deep breath before falling into the water.

Peter stayed face down in the stream holding his breath. He did his best to remain motionless as he floated to the surface holding his breath. Over the roar of the water Peter heard Ryah call his name. There was the sound of splashing which he knew would be her running through the stream towards him. After a few seconds he felt her arms around him pulling him up above the surface. She scrambled backwards and slipped sending both of them beneath the water again. Her arms wrapped around his chest again and heaved him upwards. Peter threw his arm out and grabbed her around the waist. He used the leverage to throw her back into the stream.

She stayed in the stream and looked at him in shock. The hurt was evident on her face and Peter realized that he had gone too far with is little prank. It was clear that she had been terrified. She had thought that he was drowning.

"What were you thinking?" She asked and her voice broke.

"That's the oldest trick in the book!" He said thinking of all the times that he and Ben had fooled each other as children.

"That was a cruel trick!" She said marching past him. As she walked by Peter spotted movement in the trees. He saw boots and knew that there were men standing just a few yards away from them. He grabbed her elbow as she walked past him and she spun around with a look of hatred on her face. Peter put his finger to his lips to tell her to be quiet. She must have seen his urgent expression because her mouth shut immediately. The twins who were waiting at the shore stood up and were quiet as he herded them behind one of the boulders sitting on the shore. Ryah grabbed them and pulled them down next to her. She placed one arm around each of them and they leaned against her shoulders. Peter grabbed his weapons and everything else that had been left at the shore of the stream and hurried over to drop down next to Ryah.

He selected an arrow and placed it against the bow string. He eased the string back and leaned forward to peer over the top of the boulder. Ryah sat up and squinting. The group had to be the men who had captured Ryah and Anna in the beginning. Peter knew that Ryah would recognize at least one of them. Once a man came into view she gasped. Peter took it as a sign and hoped that he would be able to defend their little group. If he could take out a few of them then maybe Thea, Petey, and Ryah could get a head start towards Chedix to warn everyone. The men on the other side of the stream looked over in their direction and Peter took aim then released the arrow just as Ryah screamed.

Chapter 4

(PETER)

Ryah shoved his arm making the arrow fly off target.

"It's Torin!" She said as she jumped to her feet, Peter watched as Ryah ran around the boulder and raced through the water holding her skirt up so her legs wouldn't get tangled in the soaked fabric. Peter watched as Torin waded through the water and caught Ryah in his open arms as she threw herself at him. Peter couldn't hear what they were saying as they held onto each other.

"Come on," Peter said to the twins. Thea was staring at Ryah and he had to nudge her shoulder to pull her back to reality. "Grab your shoes."

Petey didn't need to be told twice. He pulled his shoes on his feet. Thea sighed as she pulled her shoes on and followed Peter as he made his way into the trees.

"What's going to happen with Ryah?" Thea asked and Peter didn't answer her. Peter knew that she had been hoping that Ryah would stay with them. The little girl idolized her. They walked quietly together and as soon as they were back at home the twins ran off to go find dry clothing. Peter managed to find Ben and inform him of the approaching group. A man named Rollo was the first to arrive.

"Where is Anna?" he asked and Peter offered to take him to her.

"Is she alright?" Rollo asked and Peter assured him that his wife was just fine. After she had rested up she had started feeling better. Anna was with Ellie and the two of them were pulling in the laundry. Anna gasped when she saw her husband. Ellie managed to catch the dress that Anna dropped as she ran to meet Rollo. Rollo caught her in his arms. Anna clung to him as Rollo kissed her cheek. Peter saw the large smile on her scarred face over Rollo's shoulder.

"Are you alright?" Rollo asked again and Anna nodded. Peter felt like he was invading their moment but he couldn't take his eyes off of the couple. He could easily imagine that he was Rollo and that Ryah was Anna. He wondered what it would be like to see the woman that he loved look at him with that much love in her eyes. Rollo pulled away to kneel in front of Anna. He put his hands at her hips and leaned forward to place a kiss against her stomach. Peter started to understand Rollo's concern. Anna was pregnant. Anna blushed and she knelt down in front of her husband. She wrapped her arms around his neck and pulled him close to kiss him.

Ellie walked over to Peter and tugged on his arm to drag him inside with her. The couple deserved some privacy.

"I guess our two guests have been discovered?" Ellie said.

"It would seem so."

"Where is Ryah?"

"She's with her precious Torin," Peter spat out with more anger than he meant to.

"You knew that he would come find her."

"I didn't know that she would launch herself into his arms and hold him close. She never said anything about her relationship with him. I assumed that they were friends."

"It's usually more complicated than that," Ellie replied with a sad smile on her lips. Peter couldn't take her pity.

"I'll see you later," He said as he walked away from her. He made his way to his home which was built nearby. It was small but it was sturdy and it was all his. Ever since he had built his home he had loved how quiet and peaceful it was. But now he would give his left arm to have his own children running through the hall and his wife smiling at him as she put their supper on the table. He could already see her bright blue eyes and her shining blonde hair as she tucked it behind her ear.

Peter felt disgusted with himself for imagining that there was something there when there really wasn't anything. He pulled one of the two chairs away from his table at sat down. For a long time he glared at the single chair across from him. He didn't need two chairs. He only needed one for himself to sit in. He knew that the chair across from him would remain empty and it gnawed at him. Peter heard the bell that was ringing to signify dinner but he ignored it. The bell told him that he had been in his house for hours.

He couldn't take wallowing in his thoughts and he stood up sliding the chair back into its place against the table. He looked around at his quiet walls and made a split decision. He went to his room looking at his large empty bed and reached for the knob on his closet. He grabbed his clothes and shoved them inside the saddle bag that was draped over his chair in the corner.

He needed a change he decided as he made his way to the barn. He sucked in a deep breath of evening air as he walked. He made his way through the back door of the barn that always hung open unless there was a storm or if it was cold. "Hey Storm," Peter said as he threw his saddle bag over his horse and reached for a saddle.

"Where are you going?" Ryah's voice interrupted him as he cinched the saddle tight.

"I am leaving," he said wishing that he hadn't run into her. He wished that he had been able to escape without anyone seeing him. He had wanted to just slip away in the night without any explanations. He didn't need Ryah to see him like this.

"Why?" She asked.

"I just need to get out of here for awhile," Peter said.

"Is everything alright?" She asked and he knew that she didn't understand. He knew that she couldn't understand. She didn't feel the same way about him.

"Of course, why wouldn't it be?" He said hoping that she would drop the topic. He wished that she would just turn around and leave him alone by himself.

"Is it Torin?" Ryah asked cutting directly to the problem. Peter let out a short mocking laugh. Maybe she did understand. Maybe she did know exactly what was going on. She knew exactly what she did to him.

"He seems like more than just a 'good man," He said quoting her words from a few days earlier. Torin was clearly more than just a good man.

"Why does that matter?" She asked and he could hear the anger rising up in her voice.

"It matters because you have feelings for him," He looked her straight in the eye. He was challenging her and begging her to deny it at the same time. "You don't deny it," He whispered feeling his heart breaking. Ryah took a step away from him looking like she didn't quite know what to say. She walked away but Peter wouldn't let her get away that easily. He ran to her and caught her wrist as she tried to leave. He spun her around pinning her against the door of one of the horse stalls. He stepped up to her so he could block her escape with is body. She looked up at him with anger in her eyes.

"Let me go!" She growled but Peter didn't listen. He wanted to know what her lips tasted like. He wrapped one arm around her waist and pulled her tight against his chest. She didn't struggle. "Peter!" She warned but the sound of his name on her voice was enough to drive him to do the unthinkable. He glanced down at her lips and tilted his head to close the distance. At the last second she turned her head and his lips brushed against her cheek. He froze at her betrayal. She remained motionless in his arms with her face turned away from him like she couldn't stand the sight of him. Peter's arms dropped down at his sides and he spun away from her.

"I'm sorry," She whispered as he turned away from her and walked towards his horse. "I'm so sorry," She said a bit louder. Peter shook his head because he knew that she wasn't sorry. He knew she was just saying that to make herself feel better. He pulled himself up into his saddle and made his way towards the back door of the barn.

"Goodbye Ryah," he said then went outside. He didn't bother to look back over his shoulder. The motion of the horse and the fresh air helped to clear his head as he made his way towards the road. He didn't know where he was going but that didn't matter. All that he wanted to do was to get away from Cheddix.

<<<><><<>>>

(PETER)

Peter was leading his horse to give it a rest after the long ride. The sun was beginning to go down as he reached for the apple in his pack. He ate half of it and passed the other half to his horse. The animal munched the fruit. Peter reached back to scratch the beast between the ears. He managed to find a river for the two of them and he crouched down to scoop water up to his mouth as the horse drank freely. The horse jerked up and Peter crouched low to the water pulling the bridle down. He crouched low as he led the horse over to some of the thicker trees. He watched as Storm's ears twitched picking up sounds that were too quiet for Peter to hear.

Eventually he heard what his horse was hearing. There was the sound of footsteps. A lot of footsteps as a group made its way through the forest. The men must be the men who had abducted Ryah and Anna. He watched as the group moved. In the middle of the group there was a woman. Her dress was torn and she had thick ropes around her wrists. There was a man holding onto the end of her rope. When the man behind her reached up to brush his hand against her waist she whirled around to hit him with her tied hands. His friends laughed at her response. His arm flew through the air and collided with her face with a loud crack. She stumbled and lost her balance. She shot back to her feet.

"What are you doing?!" A voice roared and the group stopped walking. A large man made his way through the crowd. The man who had hit the girl stepped backwards as the angry man approached. "It's bad enough that the two women were lost due to incompetence, don't let anything happen to her!" He said gesturing to the woman who was tied. He grumbled something that Peter couldn't hear and with that he turned around and walked back to the front of the group.

Peter's attention was caught. He felt drawn to the girl who was tied. He wanted to be able to help her get free. He made the decision to follow the group. He followed them until it was completely dark out and he tied his horse to a tree branch. He crept through the trees trying to be as quiet as possible. He found a perfect spot to look down into the camp that had been set up. Bed rolls were set out on the ground and small fires were lit with clusters of men around them. He scanned each of the fires that he could see but he couldn't see the girl anywhere. He went a little lower and scanned the faces again. Near the fire pit in the middle of the group he spotted the man who had been holding the end of her rope from earlier. Peter searched the faces sitting around the fire but none of them were the girl. He knew that she would be somewhere nearby the man.

A few of the men produced canteens and a quiet cheer erupted. The slightly wrinkled noses and the laughter around the fire as the canteen was passed told Peter that there was alcohol. Slowly the fires crackled and burned lower and lower. New wood wasn't added and discarded empty canteens rolled across the ground. The men flopped down on their bedrolls and soon it was quiet throughout the camp. Peter took a deep breath and started making his way slowly through the sleeping men. He was careful to avoid any bodies. He didn't want anyone to know that he was there. One man groaned in his sleep and rolled over with his arm flopping down on the dirt. Slightly glowing embers from the fire offered a small amount of light for Peter to navigate the minefield of bodies. Eventually he made it to the middle. He found the man who had been holding the rope earlier and he found the rope still safely tucked in his hand.

Peter smiled and followed the rope. He picked it up and followed it to the end. He was confused when he found the end of the rope. It was frayed an uneven. He squinted at the fluffy end in confusion then a hand clapped over his mouth and a knife slipped up underneath his ribs. Peter gasped at the pain and fell to the ground.

Chapter 5

I felt a hand at my waist and I knew that it was Orvil. I spun around raising my tied hands to hit him in the face. The men around him laughed because I denied his advances. Orvil easily dodged my hands so they harmlessly grazed past him. He slapped me across the face and I stumbled backwards from the impact. I raised my hands to catch my fall but I was unsuccessful. I fell to the ground and rolled to the side jumping back to my feet before he could do anything else.

There was a commotion in the group and I knew that Kyle was making his way towards us. The men parted to let him through and Kyle stomped forward. He had a mean look on his face as he glanced at me seeing the red mark across my cheek. I knew that he wasn't worried about me. He was worried about the cargo. He wanted me to be in perfect condition when I was presented to Errit. We were just a few days away from Gareth and he wanted my old bruises to be gone by the time we got there. Anything less than perfection wouldn't be good enough for Errit.

"What are you doing?!" Kyle demanded. "It's bad enough that the two women were lost due to incompetence, don't let anything happen to her!"

He grumbled about the stupidity of his men then walked back up to his place in the front of the group.

I had pieced together bits and pieces about the two women from earlier that he had mentioned. The two women were a gift for Errit. They had killed Errits beloved sister Grey when she left home to go see her betrothed to get married. Grey was attacked by a jealous woman and she was killed. Errit had vowed to seek his revenge on his sisters killer so he abducted the wife of Grey's betrothed. She had been taken with her handmaiden and the two of them started their journey to Gareth. Before they could make it to Gareth the women were taken by the Red Demon. Kyle took his men after the Red Demon but the stories of the men that the Red Demon had killed were too much for many of Kyle's men. Many men ran off in the night leaving Kyle about twenty five men under his control. With that few men it would be difficult to get the women back from the Red Demon. Kyle decided to find a new woman instead because Errit wouldn't know the difference anyway.

I sighed as I fell into step with the men around me. I had been in the wrong place a the wrong time. Now I was going to be a gift for the leader of Gareth. Many of the men told me that I should be honored but I didn't feel honored.

I walked for the rest of the day keeping pace with the men. It was getting darker and colder. I tried to wrap my arms around myself to keep warm but it didn't make much of a difference. Kyle stopped our march as he declared our location fit for the night. I was grateful for the news and I sunk down to the ground. Henrich was the man holding my rope. He looked at me where I was sitting and he rolled his eyes but he didn't make me move. Five fire pits were thrown together and soon there were warm fires crackling away. I watched from the end of my rope as the sparks flew up into the air. I was too far away to feel the heat and there wasn't any room for me to squeeze in between the men. I didn't want to get close to them anyways. I could imagine the crude comments and the lingering looks that would be sent my way. Even though I was cold I felt better where I was.

I watched as a canteen was produced from thin air. The men laughed as it was passed around. Other fires around the camp had similar canteens that were being passed. I wondered where the limitless supply of alcohol came from.

Each man took a long swig of the drink. I knew that it would be alcohol. The men loved their alcohol at night and they would regret it the next morning. I knew they would get slightly drunk and I dreaded the behavior that could come from the drink. I had already seen the behavior back home. I knew what it did to a man and the things that he could do. The next day would be full of tears and meaningless 'I'm sorrys'. I watched as one of the men leaned back against his bed roll with a sloppy smile on his face. His eyes were already closed. An idea started creeping into my mind as I watched the men slowly slip deeper into their drunken state.

When Henrich fell under the induced sleep I crawled forward. I knew that he would keep a dagger nearby. I wrinkled my nose as I thought about searching for the knife. I didn't want to touch him. He shifted slightly and the dying embers of the fire caught the light of something shiny at his belt. I reached for it searching for a handle and I wasn't disappointed.

I squinted through the darkness to make sure that he was still asleep before I slid the dagger away from his belt. I crept back to my place at the end of the rope and started sawing awkwardly at the knots at my wrist. Pushing my torn skirts out of the way I managed to hold the handle between my feet and slide the ropes up and down the blade. Using as much force as I dared I sliced through the thick ropes slowly. After a few moments I was finally free. Once I was free I stood up rubbing my sore wrists. I looked around to make sure that all of the men were still happily asleep. When I saw a man standing nearby I nearly screamed in fright. He walked to the fire and looked around at the sleeping faces. When he found Henrich he spotted the rope that he had in his hand. I watched as the man leaned down to pick up the rope. Holding it in his hands he started following it out. I took a few steps back until I bumped into a tree. The man kept walking and I knew that he was looking for me. I knew that he expected me to be at the end of the rope. He had waited for all of the men to get drunk then he had come for me. I knew that it would be Orvil. I had humiliated him earlier and now he was going to search me out in the darkness.

The man finally reached the end of the rope and he paused. I knew that he was looking at the end of the rope. It had clearly been cut. I knew that any second he was going to sound the alarm that I was gone and I would be discovered. There was no way that I would be able to get away from twenty five men even if they were slightly drunk. I took a deep breath as I thought about my freedom and I silently moved forward grasping the dagger in my hand. I got behind the man and clapped my hand over his mouth and slid the dagger up underneath his ribs just like my older brother had shown me.

The man didn't even struggle as he slumped to the ground. I hoped that he was dead as I made my way out of the camp with long strides. I hoped to never see any of the horrible men again. I should have known that I wouldn't be that lucky. A hot hand closed around my wrist and I was yanked backwards. My gasp froze on my lips as a hand clapped over my mouth.

"Where do you think you're going?" Orvil's hot breath fanned over my neck. I pulled away from him but he didn't let go. His hand remained on my mouth as he pulled me along away from the sleeping men. I knew better than to make a sound and risk waking up someone else. Dealing with Orvil would be bad enough. I didn't need anyone else awake. I allowed him to guide me out of the camp. "This should be far enough," He said once we were away. He brushed my hair away from my neck and pressed his lips against my shoulder. Everything inside me was screaming. I could feel my skin crawl at his disgusting touch. Slowly his hand moved away from my mouth and went to my waist turning me around to face him. "Now this won't be so bad," he whispered in between kisses. He wrapped both of his arms around me pulling me close.

I closed my eyes and drove my knee upwards. He hissed in pain and released me dropping to the ground. I didn't wait to see how long he stayed there. I took off sprinting as fast as I could. I wanted to put as much space between me and Orvil as possible. My foot caught on a root which caused me to stumble. I picked myself up and kept going. I didn't know where I was going. It didn't matter where I went. My lungs were burning when I finally slowed down. I could barely hear the sound of water over my breathing and my pounding heart. I knew that there must be a stream nearby. I followed the sound and dropped to my knees scooping up a handful of the water and quickly drinking. I bent down to scoop up more water.

"You shouldn't have done that!" I heard Orvil hiss just before I felt his hand sink into the hair at the back of my head. He grabbed a handful and shoved my face down into the water. A soundless scream erupted around me in a cloud of bubbles. I kicked and punched but it was worthless. Orvil pulled me out of the water and I coughed and spluttered as I tried to suck in a breath of air. He wrapped an arm around my waist hauling me up with his other hand still clutching my hair. He took a step froward into the deeper water and dunked me down again before I could get a big breath of air. I sucked in water. My lungs burst with pain and I tried to cough but it was useless. Cold black water engulfed me. A stream should have been a life force in the forest but I knew that it was about to kill me. The water slowed my movements as I fought for just one more breath.

Suddenly, Orvil's strong hold was gone.

I tried to grab a footing on the bottom of the stream and finally got myself upright pushing my hair out of my face to suck in air. All of the air that I managed to breath in seemed to get coughed right back out. But it didn't matter. I was breathing again. I clawed my way up to the bank of the water and flopped down on my stomach with my mouth wide open to suck in the cool night air. I opened my eyes to see Orvil trapped in a headlock. I could see a strong arm around his neck but I couldn't see the man behind him. He was just going to get Orvil out of the way so he could get to me. I should have been running away but I just didn't care. All that mattered was getting another breath of air. Orvil dropped down to his knees and the man behind him followed him down to the ground without breaking his hold. The light from the moon caught his face and I didn't recognize him. He wasn't one of the men in Kyle's company. I stared at Orvil's face as his eyes rolled up back into his head. He was completely still and the man let him flop to the ground. I stared at Orvil's motionless face. His mouth was hanging open and his eyes were slightly open. He wasn't moving.

I remembered about the man who had pulled Orvil off of me and I looked up at his face. He was kneeling over Orvil and he was breathing heavily. I glanced down to see that he was covered in blood. The blood was coming from a familiar looking wound. He was the man who I had stabbed. He had just saved me. He got one leg underneath him and tried to push himself up but he just sagged back down to the ground. He didn't say a word as he fell down to the side unconscious. I stared at him unable to process what I had just seen.

A nicker from a horse made me jump as the large animal walked forward out of the darkness to the man laying in front of me. It leaned down and brushed its nose over the man's face nudging him. When he didn't move the horse made the same noise again. I was worried that it would make too much noise. I got up to my feet and stumbled over to the animal. I held my hand out and it allowed me to approach slowly. I reached up and rubbed its forehead as I picked up its reins that had been dragging on the ground.

I looked at the horse and then down at the man laying at my feet. I knew what I had to do.

Chapter 6

(LYDIA)

I used the dagger to slice the shirt off of the bleeding man at my feet. The fabric stuck to the warm sticky blood that was oozing from the wound that I had inflicted. With each breath that he took his chest moved up and down which caused more blood to ooze. I squinted at the wound and I knew that I had missed anything major. I knew that my brother would be disappointed in me. I was just a hair away from nicking the major vessel. This man in front of me was extremely lucky. If my aim had been true he would have bled out in just a few seconds I tore off a section of my skirt and used it to mop up the blood so that I could see. Once I found the major source of the bleeding I tore another section of my skirt and dipped it into the stream. I folded it up and placed it on his wound. I knew that pressure would help stop the bleeding. I knew that he would probably need to have it sewn up if it was going to heal properly.

I looked down at my skirt which was in an awful state. There were so many holes in the dirty fabric that it was difficult to find a piece that would work as a bandage. I found a relatively large chunk that wasn't full of holes and I tore it free. I hooked my arms around his chest and pulled him into a sitting position with him leaning heavily on me. I nearly lost my balance. Falling would pin me underneath him. I managed to grab the wrap that I had made and slid it around his torso. It went around twice and I tied it tightly to hold his bandage in place.

He hadn't regained consciousness which was probably for the best. If he was awake he would only be in a lot of pain. I eased him back down to the ground laying on his back. The man's horse nickered and I hoped that the animal would cooperate with me. I slowly approached it with my hands held out at my sides. With a twitching nose the horse watched as I approached. It took a step towards me and I slowly held my hand out to it and scratched its nose. Reins hung down from a bridle so I took them in my hand and led the horse back to the man laying on the ground. It leaned down to smell its master.

"I need your help," I whispered and the silky ears twitched.

<<<><><>>>

(LYDIA)

I held tightly onto the reins. The injured man was laying behind me across the back of his horse. I had to remove the saddle and lean forward to make room for him. I pointed the horse in the direction of home. I knew how to get there but I was afraid of getting caught again. I followed the road closely watching for hidden trails that would take me home.

I stopped to check the man's wound. The bandage seemed to be holding. I glanced around to make sure that we weren't being followed. We had ridden for most of the day and I knew that we were getting close to my town. I wondered if anyone would notice that I was gone. When my father went outside he would see that the animals hadn't been taken care of. It wouldn't matter that I had been abducted. All that he would care about would be my chores not being neglected. I sighed and swung back up onto the horse. I could worry about his reaction later.

After a few more minutes of riding my town came into view. First, it was the well kept house of Eliza. She had a kind heart and often looked out for me when my father got out of control. I knew that I could slip over to her house and find a fresh cake. Eliza would listen to me and ease my worries. Many times she had offered to let me move into her home with her. The offer was tempting but I knew that she would be putting herself at risk. I made an excuse by telling her that we would be too cramped in her little home. She had pursed her lips as she shook her head slowly at me. I didn't want her to get hurt. I could handle it if my father hurt me but if he hurt Eliza because of me I didn't know what I would do.

I looked around at the other houses as I approached. I could imagine the shutters on the windows locking tightly. I could imagine rain falling down from the sky drenching me and making my thin clothes stick to my body. The reason for me being outside was always the same. I could remember the way that my father had roared at me shaking his fists when he was in a drunken rage. My neighbors always slammed their shutters tight when they saw me coming. It didn't matter the season of the year. It could be sweltering hot outside and they would slam their shutters and close their doors. Many times I imagined their houses as little ovens and I hoped that they would bake inside them. My only neighbor and friend who was a refuge from the storm was Eliza.

Today was a different story. My neighbors were outside working in their gardens or beating rugs that were strung over lines. They looked up at me on my horse with wide eyes as they saw the man strung over the saddle behind me. Many of them looked curious but I didn't stop for an explanation. I kept riding with my end goal in sight. There was a home just ahead that belonged to a man skilled in medicine. He claimed that he wasn't a doctor but he had a gift for healing. I could think of many occasions where his gift came in handy.

I pulled the horse to a stop and dropped down into the dirt road outside of his house. Little puffs of dust fluttered up around my feet when I touched down. I glanced at the man behind me to make sure that he was still breathing. Once I was sure that he was still alive I jumped up the step in front of me and knocked on the door with a closed fist.

The door opened up in front of me and James looked at me I saw his eyebrows lift in surprise then he glanced over my shoulder. His eyebrows lifted farther and he slipped around me to hurry towards the man. He untied him and together we lifted him off of the horse and carried him inside.

"What happened to him?" James asked.

"I stabbed him," I said slowly as we lifted the man up onto the table that served as a bed. His head rolled slightly to the side and his forehead wrinkled in pain.

James shook his head at my explanation and started to examine the piece of cloth that I had wrapped around the man's chest. He cut through the fabric and let it fall to the table. He peeled away the cloth pad that I had used to try to stop the bleeding.

"Well done," He mumbled under his breath as he examined the wound. Blood oozed now that the pad had been pulled away. "This will need to be stitched. He said as he dabbed at the blood. I went to where he kept his supplies. I had been in his home enough times to know where he kept his belongings. He had sewed me up enough times in the past. He took the bag of supplies and rummaged through it until he came across what he was looking for.

"Your father has been in here looking for you," he mumbled as he set to work.

"Oh, really?" I asked as I perched on one of his chairs.

"He has gotten better hasn't he?" James asked and I knew that he was right. My father wasn't perfect but he had gotten better since my mother had died. He used to beat us daily. He would come home drunk and he would beat my mother. Then he would beat me. The next day he would be sweet and sorry as he tried to make it up to us. There would be fresh wild flowers on the table and he would comb his hair and put on a nice shirt. At dinner he would slide our chairs out for us and offer to help clean up the dishes. A few days latter he would come home drunk and the cycle would start over again. Many times my mother would yell for me to leave. I knew that it would make things worse for her but as a child I was a coward. I didn't want to see her get hurt. I didn't want to listen to her cries. Every time she would tell me to run I would obey. I was always worried when I would come home the next morning. Would my mother be dead? Would my father be passed out in the yard? I remembered tip toeing through the yard in my thin night dress as the fear would rise up and clutch at my throat.

I would pause on the front step and take a few deep breaths to steady myself. The handle on the door was always cold making my skin tingle and a shiver roll down my spine as I would clutch it. The door would open slowly because I was too scared to open it quickly. Looking inside was always the most difficult part. I always imagined the worst and anticipated finding it.

"Yes, he has gotten better." I replied as I came back to reality. There were still rough days but things were much better than they had been when I was a child. The death of my mother gave my father a wake up call and he wasn't nearly as violent as he had been. He started drinking less frequently.

He would only be violent occasionally. I folded my arms around my waist and waited for James to finish stitching the man up on his table.

"He should probably stay here for a few days," James said as he tied a knot in the thread. "I can keep an eye on him and make sure that his wound is healing properly."

I nodded in understanding and stood up from my chair with my arms still wrapped around myself. James glanced down at my tattered dress. His eyes wandered up until they met mine and I saw sadness and pity. In the past many people had suggested that James and I make a union. He was many years my senior and would be considered a good match and a husband. As I looked at the sadness and pity in his eyes I knew why it would never work between us. I could never marry a man who pitied me. I could never marry a man who saw me as weak and not his equal. James would be an excellent match, for someone else.

"Thank you for your help," I said giving him a smile.

"My pleasure, Lydia," He said. I walked around him and out his front door. I glanced back to the man lying on the table. His blonde hair was slick with sweat and he had blood on him. He was muscular but right now he was vulnerable. I didn't know the man at all but I wanted him to live.

I pulled my eyes away from the man and walked out the front door towards his horse. I climbed up into the saddle and positioned my skirt around my legs as best as I could. My father would be unhappy if he saw the state that I was traveling in. I didn't think that he would care much about the fact that I had been abducted or that I had been in danger.

"Let's go home," I whispered the horse.

Chapter 7

(LYDIA)

I could see my father sitting out front of our house in his old rocking chair. He didn't alter his rocking pace as he watched me ride into the yard. His expression didn't change as he looked at my appearance. He didn't ask questions about the unfamiliar horse that I was riding.

"Where have you been?" He asked.

I didn't reply to him for a few seconds as I tried to think of what to say to him. I knew that it wouldn't matter what was said. I could have said that I ran away or that I secretly married. His reaction would be the same. "I was abducted by a group of men when I went to get water at the stream."

"You neglected to do your chores," He said as he rocked back and forth in his chair.

I shook my head slowly and dropped down off of the horse. I pulled the animal behind me and led it to the barn. We had a few empty stalls where it could be kept. My father would be more concerned with the lost bucket that I had dropped when the men had grabbed me from behind. I could remember the feel of the thick arms that wrapped around me. I shivered at the thought and led the horse towards the barn.

"Don't you walk away from me while I am talking to you!" My father growled behind me. I heard his footsteps approach and I felt his hand as he roughly grabbed my arm forcing me to spin around and face him. He leaned down to get into my face. When he was just inches from me he stopped as he glared into my eyes. I hated that I had his eyes. I wanted nothing to do with him yet I inherited one of his most prominent features. His blue eyes glared into mine like a mirror image. I felt like I was looking into my own soul and all that I could see was darkness. I tried to pull my arm away from his grasp which made him tighten his hand. I could feel my hand and lower arm start to tingle from the lack of blood flow.

I stood there and looked straight into my father eyes as he glared at me. For the first time he seemed to see the dirt smudges and bruises on my face. He noticed the tangled state of my hair and my shredded dress. He released my arm one finger at a time and I pulled it close to my body for protection.

"Get on with your chores," He growled then stomped back across the yard and plopped down in his chair. The creak of the wood let me know that he was rocking back and forth again. I knew that he wouldn't care that I had gone missing but that didn't make it hurt any less. I walked into the dark barn and pulled the door shut behind me. Once inside, I went to open the windows to allow the slight breeze to come through with the sunlight.

The day at the stream when the men had gagged me had been just a few days ago. I remembered it perfectly. A gag had been tied around my mouth to keep me quiet. I punched and kicked until a silver knife appeared in front of my face. When I stopped struggling the man threw me over his shoulder and carried me through the trees.I remembered when he had dropped me to my feet in front of Kyle. Kyle untied the gag and I screamed loudly earning a slap across the face that was so hard my head snapped back and I saw spots. The slap was similar to ones that I had received back at home.

I looked down at my wrists which were still raw from the ropes that had been tied around them. I rubbed the sore skin as I thought about being led through miles of the forest with a group of men who were similar to my father. They had been violent and mean. Kyle's influence had protected me from the men with the worst of intentions but that didn't mean that I had enjoyed my journey.

I glanced around at the familiar walls around me to remind myself that I was home and for the moment I was fairly safe. I felt a trickle of a tear on my face and I reached up to wipe it off with the back of my hand. I looked at the tear on my hand and tried to remember the last time that I had cried. Crying made my father angrier and so I learned not to cry. Thinking of what had happened shouldn't drive me to such a weak emotion. I led the horse into a stall and took the saddle off. I found a brush and started to work.

The monotony of the movements helped to clear my head. I thought about the new stranger that James was helping. I knew now that when he had grabbed me at the campsite he was just trying to help me. I had stabbed him with the intention of killing him but I had been unsuccessful. Even after my attempt to kill him he had still come to my rescue to save me. The more I thought about him the more I wondered about him. I knew that James would do everything in his power to help the new stranger. I finished brushing the horse and I started taking care of the other animals that were in the barn.

Their pails of food and water were empty and dry. It was my responsibility to fill them so my father didn't even bother with it. The animals could have been near starvation and he would have left them because it wasn't his responsibility to take care of them. He would sit in his chair and rock back and forth. I peeked through the window and saw him rocking on the front porch with a vacant look on his wrinkled face. I tried to imagine him younger.

I remembered when I was younger and my mother would describe the early days when she had met my father. She talked about a kind man who loved life. Most of all he loved her and his children. They had started a life together and created a family. My older brother was born and I followed a few years later. My mother described those years as the happiest in her life. Then things started to change. My father got 'sick' as my mother called him and he grew abusive and violent. At the age of sixteen my brother left home never to be seen again. I was eleven as I stood on the front porch and begging him not to go. He reached down and played with one of my braids like he had always done. He used it to tickle my cheek. I laughed and he smiled then he glanced up and I knew that my father was behind me.

"I have to go," My brother said then he walked off of the porch. I watched him walk up the dusty road I didn't know that he was walking out of my life forever and that I wouldn't ever see him again. I remembered how he had secretly taught me to use a knife at the age of nine. I wondered if he hoped that I would use it on father. A few years later mother got sick and she died.

The people from town had gathered around my father and I as a flimsy wooden coffin was lowered into rich brown dirt. They had patted me on the head and told me that everything would be alright. They didn't know about the nightmare that I was living at home. They didn't know that my father was the reason that my mother was dead. They thought that our lives were as happy as the cheerful yellow curtains that my mother had hung in the window. I remember her saying that they would liven up the kitchen and brighten our lives. All they did was block out the stares of curious eyes if people happened to be nearby when my father came home in a drunken rage.

The back door of the barn opened pulling me from my thoughts.

"Good morning, beautiful," Ruben said as he poked his face inside and caught me lost in thought.

"Hello," I said with a smile that would cover up what I was really feeling.

"Where have you been?"

"I went to visit my aunt Gladys in the country," I lied. For some reason I didn't want to tell Ruben where I had really been. I didn't want him to ask questions that I didn't want to answer or think about.

"And how is she doing?" He asked as he walked towards me. I turned around to face him and he rested his arms on the stall behind me leaning in with his arms around me.

"She is doing well," I replied.

"Is that so?" He asked leaning in to press his lips gently against mine.

"Yes," I answered as he pulled away and rested his forehead against mine.

"I would like to meet this Aunt Gladys of yours."

"She is a wonderful woman," I said. Gladys had died many years ago but Ruben didn't know that. He didn't know very much about me. He claimed to love me which made me wonder how I felt about him. My father also liked Ruben and thought that he would be a good match for me. Ruben's father was rich and well known by the community. I had met him many times when I had gone into the bar to haul my father outside and bring him home. Ruben's father was one of my father's best friends. He was a lot like my father and that was what concerned me.

"She would have to be a wonderful woman, she is related to you."

I laughed at his remark and gently pushed him away. He caught my hand with his and used it to pull me forward against him. His arms wrapped around me and I let my arms fall to my sides.

"I missed you," Ruben whispered and kissed me again with passion. I allowed the kiss to go farther than normal without pushing him away. Part of me wondered just how far he would take it. He groaned and pulled away taking a few steps away from me. He leaned against the stall opposite of me and caught his breath. He looked back to me and gave a chuckle. "It's good to have you back."

"It's good to be back," I said.

"Why did you go in the first place?" He asked. He always asked me questions like this. He wanted to constantly know where I was and what I was doing. There were a lot of times when I would leave Eliza's house and he would surprise me by being there to walk me home. Ruben never asked me about the bruises that my father would leave on my skin. I knew that it was because he didn't want to embarrass me.

"My Aunt Gladys was sick and I went to take care of her."

"Hopefully you don't catch anything. You should really let the doctor go and have a look at her instead of you next time."

"Next time I will," I replied as I picked up the empty feed buckets and went to fill them out of the large sacks in the corner. Ruben didn't move as he examined the large new guest that was munching on hay. I heaved the buckets back to the stalls and hung them to feed the animals. I collected the empty pails of water and went to the back door of the barn pushing it open with my back because my hands were full with the buckets. Ruben followed me out to the stream. I looked around at the edge of the water to see if there was any sign of what had happened a few days ago. I wanted to see if there were footprints in the sad to let me know the direction that my attackers had come from.

The recent rain that had come through had washed away any sign of a struggle. I hoped to find my lost bucket that had been dropped when I was grabbed but it was nowhere to be found. I filled my buckets with the fresh water and made the slow trip back to the barn. I didn't want any of the water to slosh out of the full buckets. By the time the barn came into view my shoulders were aching from the weight. I had to set one of my buckets down to get the back door of the barn open. Once it was open I held it open with my foot and bent to pick up the bucket then made my way inside the barn.

I lifted the large buckets and dumped them into the water trough for the horses. Each horse had its own trough and needed two buckets to fill it completely. Ruben followed me inside and then when I went back out I held the door open for him as he followed close behind me. With two buckets I made three more trips from the stream to fill all of the water troughs for the animals.

I started cleaning out their stalls after their food and water was full. Ruben leaned against the stall doors talking to me as I worked. Once I was finished I checked all of the animals to make sure that they were alright. Then I went to the chicken coop to check for eggs. There were six good eggs and three that were smashed letting me know that my father hadn't bothered to check for eggs in the time that I had been gone. I hadn't expected him to check them because gathering the eggs was my responsibility. I held the eggs in what was left of the skirt of my dress and walked towards the house.

My father continued to rock back and forth with his blank stare as I went past him into the house. It was dark inside and smelled musty. I opened the shutters on the windows to let the light in and I wished that I hadn't. The kitchen was a disaster. I could tell from the looks of things that my father had spent at least one of the nights drinking. When he had returned home with nothing to hit he started destroying the house. Ruben walked in behind me and paused in the doorway looking at the destruction. He sucked in a large breath and I felt my face heat up. I was so tired of making excuses for my father's behavior. He acted like a small child not getting his way.

"Well, I best be going," Ruben said he stepped forward to place a kiss on my cheek then he turned on heel and he was gone, leaving me to clean up the mess.

Chapter 8

(LYDIA)

The sun set and my father wandered into the house. He walked past me as I scrubbed at a large stain on the floor. He flopped down into bed without another sound. I had cooked him supper a few hours ago then continued to clean the mess in the kitchen. The moon was high in the sky when I threw out my last bucket of dirty water.

I wiped my filthy face on my sleeve and went out to check on the animals one last time. The new horse in the stable perked up when I walked in. I went to scratch the horse between the ears. I knew that it was wondering where its master was. Once I was satisfied with everything I went back into the house and climbed the ladder to my loft bedroom. It was small but that suited me just fine. I didn't bother to take of my disgusting clothes. I was too exhausted. I sat down on the edge of my bed and rolled to my side. Within a few seconds I was asleep.

The sun rose high in the sky in what felt like just a few minutes later. I sat up slowly and stretched my achy muscles. I rubbed my eyes to clear the sleep out of them. I went to the basin that was in the corner and splashed some of the water that I had replaced last night up on my face. I peeled my destroyed dress off of my shoulders and used a wet rag to clean myself up a bit. Once I was somewhat clean I went to the closet and found another dress. This dress had been my mothers and though it was worn it was still a pretty gown. It was blue and there were small roses in the design. I had trimmed the thin lace off of the collar to make it a better work gown. My mother treasured the lace so I had sewed it onto the collar of my Sunday dress instead. Once I was dressed for the day I went downstairs to the kitchen to start on breakfast for my father.

Everything looked a lot better today than it had last night. Everything was in its place. I started up the fire and placed eggs in a pan to scramble up for my father's breakfast. I put some of the left over jam on a piece of bread for him. He lumbered into the kitchen and took his plate off of the table. Then he walked outside and plopped down in his chair. I could hear the steady creak of the wood from his rocker.

"This bread is stale!" He yelled in at me and I heard him drop it on the porch refusing to eat it. I looked at what was left of the bread which was only a heel which would be my breakfast. I scrapped the last bit of the jam out of the jar and spread it across the bread. Then I cleaned up the breakfast dishes. I went out to collect his plate and I looked down at the bread that he had thrown on the porch. It was useless now.

"I will make more bread today Papa," I said.

"You should have made bread yesterday," He grumbled.

I didn't say anything as I got his plate and went inside to wash it. I was going to go to town to check on James and his patient. Once I was finished with the dishes I went outside and picked up the discarded bread off of the porch and went to toss it into the chicken coop.

"At least you girls don't care if the bread is a bit stale," I whispered to them as their happy clucking filled my ears. I ate my breakfast as I walked into town. There was a large tree growing in a neighbor's yard with branches that extended into the street. I could see peach dangling off of the branch. I checked to see if the neighbor was in sight and when I didn't see them I reached up for the fruit. I wished for a knife to peel off the fuzzy layer of the peach. I knew that James would have one so I slipped the fruit into my pocket as I walked. A few minutes later I could see his house.

I didn't bother to knock because I knew that James would be out with his other patients. I let myself into his house and nearly crashed into the man standing on the other side of the door. He was knocked off balance and fell to the floor groaning and rolling to his side in pain. I gasped at the sudden collision and realized that the man was the man that I had stabbed.

I dropped down to his side. "Are you alright?!" I gasped as I tried to get him to look at me.

He finally met my gaze with pain in his eyes.

"Are you the girl who stabbed me?" He winced.

"Yes," I replied as I crouched down.

"I thought so," He said as he laid flat on the ground with his eyes tightly shut. He looked pale. I sat down next to him because I didn't know what else to do for him. He opened his eyes a crack and squinted at me. "I'm alright," He breathed I knew that he was trying to comfort me.

"You don't look alright," I replied.

"I have you to thank for that it would seem."

"I am sorry for stabbing you, I thought that you were someone else."

"I am glad to hear that you don't stab all the men that you meet."

"Just the ones that startle me in the night."

"I'll keep that in mind," He said as he opened his eyes farther and tried to sit up.

"You probably shouldn't do that!" I said putting my hand on his shoulder to push him back down. "James will be back soon and he will help you get back into bed."

"Is James your husband?" He asked.

"No he is the doctor. I brought you to him for him to help you get better."

"After you stabbed me? First you try to kill me then you try to save me."

"That seems to be the case."

He gave a short laugh then clutched at his chest because it hurt too much to laugh.

"I am sorry that I tried to kill you. I didn't realize that you were trying to help me."

"Apology accepted. Maybe you can help me get back into bed."

"I don't think that it would be a good idea," I said but he was already trying to sit up. I didn't think it would be that much different from helping my father. I scooted closer to him and helped him put his arm around my shoulders. I hooked an arm around his waist and got my legs underneath myself and tried to stand up. He grunted and hissed in pain on the way up but I got him standing. He closed his eyes and he looked even paler once he was upright.

"Thank you," He whispered and we slowly made it to the bed that was in the corner. I eased him down and lowered him down onto the straw mattress. He opened his eyes to give me a smile in appreciation. "Could you get me something to drink?" He asked quietly.

"Of course," I replied slipping out from underneath his arm and hurrying to the kitchen. I opened the cupboard and found a few of the cups. James was lucky enough to have a spout in his kitchen. I hurried over to it and lifted the handle. The water gurgled up and the water splashed down into the sink. I put the cup underneath it and filled it. After shutting off the water I took the cup to the man.

"Thank you, again," He said accepting the cup and drinking it. "I don't even know your name," He said as he passed me back the empty cup.

"It's Lydia," I replied.

"My name is Peter," He said as he leaned back against the bed.

"It's nice to meet you Peter."

"What have you learned about our new patient?" James asked causing me to jump because I hadn't heard him come in.

I stood up from the edge of the bed and went to speak with James across the room.

"His name is Peter, I gave him some water to drink I hope that is alright."

"Where did you find him?"

"He was trying to leave. I opened the door and ran into him. He fell down so I helped him up and I got him over to the bed."

"He will need to get some more rest and I think that he should stay here for a few more days." James said and I nodded. "How is your father doing?"

"He is the same." I said as I rubbed my arm where underneath my sleeve there was a bruise from where he had grabbed me yesterday.

"If you ever need anything, you do have a place here." James said gesturing to the four walls around us. I tried to hide my shocked expression.

"Thank you," I said standing up and heading towards the door. "I'll come back tomorrow to check on Peter," I said liking the sound of his name. Now we didn't have to just call him the patient or the man that was hurt.

"He will be here." James said and I nodded as I walked out the front door and made my way down the street. I was going to head home but instead I decided to go towards Eliza's house. I followed the familiar path ignoring the houses on the side of the street. The people living in the houses had ignored me enough times in the past. I kept my head held high and walked straight to Eliza's. She was outside her house sitting on her front porch. Her eyes were closed as she rocked back and forth in her chair. I slipped through her front gate and tiptoed up her cobblestone walk way.

"You're getting quieter," She said softly.

"I don't know how you do that?!" I said stomping my foot. Eliza always seemed to hear me when I was trying to sneak up on her. She laughed and held her hand out to me as I got closer.

"Let me take a look at you darling," She said and I paused for her inspection. "You look tired."

"I am tired."

"What happened to you?"

"I went on a journey and got back later than I expected."

She gave my hand a squeeze letting me know that she didn't believe me but she didn't push me farther than that. Using my hand she pulled herself upright to stand in front of me.

"Let's go inside and get some breakfast," She said. She always insisted that I didn't get enough to eat and she was usually right. I remembered the peach in my pocket so I pulled it out and offered it to her. She picked it up in her wrinkled hand and brought it close to her nose and inhaled deeply. "I have some fresh milk that will go perfectly with this."

I found a knife and set to work slicing the fuzzy peel off of the fruit. Once it was gone I sliced it into small pieces. Eliza returned with a small pitcher of milk that was given to her daily by a neighbor boy that she practically raised. She placed a bowl in front of me and filled it with half of the slices of the peach and poured the fresh milk over it. I took it from her and we ate together.

"Is that Ruben boy still bothering you?" She asked after she wiped her mouth on a large cloth napkin that was sitting next to her bowl.

I thought about the way that he had caught me in the barn. The feel of his lips moving against mine. He was the only boy that I had kissed. I didn't know anything different from Ruben's advances.

"I wouldn't call it 'bothering' me," I said and she threw her napkin at me. I caught it before it could hit me directly in the face.

"That boy is trouble."

I knew how she felt about Ruben. I didn't know how I felt about him. I knew that I didn't love him but that didn't make him a bad person.

"You should be careful around him," She warned me for what felt like the tenth time.

"I will be careful around him."

"Now tell me about this other man that you brought into town yesterday?"

I looked up at her shocked.

"I saw you riding into town on a new horse with a large man draped over the back of the saddle. Where did you find him and what did you do with him?"

"I stabbed him out in the forest. Then I decided to bring him home to be healed. He is with James right now."

"You stabbed him?" She asked.

I knew that she would believe me about being kidnapped but I didn't want to worry her. I knew that she worried about me enough with my father I didn't need to give her another reason to worry about me.

"He looked handsome. If you asked me I would have said that you should have kissed him instead of stabbing him!"

Chapter 9

- -

(LYDIA)

It had been a few days since I had been in to see Peter. I wondered how he was doing but I knew that James would take excellent care of him. The day had been a hot one and so I had all of the windows wide open hoping to catch a breeze. All of the shutters were tied back and the few windows that actually still had glass in them were open as well. I could remember when all of the windows had glass. Many of them hadn't survived my father's fits.

I wiped sweat off of my forehead with the sleeve at my forearm and continued working on dinner. I heard a noise outside so I glanced up through the window that was in front of me. Ruben was just a few inches away from my face making me jump.

"What are you doing?!" I gasped as I felt my heart jump up in my throat.

"Just watching a pretty girl," he replied as he leaned forward to rest his forearms on the window sill.

I blushed and glanced down to the dough that I had been kneading. It was going to be for dinner tonight. I saw Ruben glance down at the bread too. We didn't have much but I knew that it would be rude to not offer to share.

"You always make the best bread," He said dreamily and I looked up at him smiling at his compliment.

"Would you like to stay for supper?" I asked.

"I would love to!" Ruben said as he reached forward to caress my face through the open window. "I need to go talk to your father about something," he said then turned and walked to the front porch where my father would be sitting. I sighed and continued with my work shaping the loaf so that it would fit into the pan.

Once it was the correct size and shape I left it in the pan to raise while I went to see to my other chores. With an extra person I would have to stretch the already thin soup even farther. I glanced around at the cupboards that were emptying quickly. I would need to go into town very soon to fill up on supplies. I smiled because it would give me another chance to stop in and check on Peter's progress.

I could hear the mumble of voices out front which made me want to go listen but I knew that it would be rude so I set to work busying myself with other things. Going out the back door I made my way to the barn. The horses perked up at the sound of my entrance and their large ears twitched as I started talking to them. I knew that they wanted to get out but I didn't have time right now to take them for a ride. Peter's horse looked at me expectantly.

"Your master should be well soon," I said to the animal as I scratched her ears and stroked her soft nose. "I am sure that you miss him, he is probably a lot more fun than I am." I glanced at the food and water levels making sure that everything was still full. I had a few hours before my bread would be ready so I opened the doors of the stall and led her out into the yard into the large corral.

She walked around stretching her legs after being in the stall for the day. I wanted to put a saddle on the horse and go for a ride but Ruben didn't like it when I took a horse out. He always said that it was too dangerous and that I could get hurt. He was always worried about my safety. I looked at the horse and then glanced back at my father and Ruben on the porch. They were deep in conversation. I could probably get away for a small ride. I pulled the horse back into the barn and found the saddle.

Once she was ready to go I climbed up onto her tall back and made my way out the back door of the barn hoping to get away before I was seen. I didn't look back over my shoulder once as I went out of the yard in the direction of town. Once we were on the road I could tell that the horse was impatient. I leaned forward and held tight as we took off at a run. It felt like we were soaring over the ground. The sound of hooves let me know that we were still on the path instead of flying through the air. My hair whipped around my shoulders streaming out behind me. My dress hitched up as I held my feet in the stirrups and gripped the reins.

If Ruben were here and could see me now I knew that he would be furious. But he wasn't here now and he couldn't see me. I let Peter's horse run just as fast as she wanted to. Within a few short minutes we were in town. I reined her in for the sake of appearances. I dropped down off of her back and made sure that my dress had dropped back down into its place. I ran a hand over my hair hoping that it would be enough to smooth it down.

I knocked on the doctor's door to let him know that I was there then I opened the door slowly letting myself in. I half expected to run into Peter again but instead I found him sitting on a chair at the table while James examined him. There was a neat little row of stitches beneath the edge of Peter's ribs.

"Good afternoon, Lydia," James said without looking up from his work.

"Hello James, Peter," I nodded at Peter when he looked up at me and smiled.

"It's good to see you again," Peter said enthusiastically as the doctor continued to examine him seriously. James was always serious in his work and paid expert attention to all of the details. I walked forward and sat down at one of the free chairs at the table.

I could see the stitches in Peter's chest and they reminded me of a time not so long ago. It had been raining that night. I remembered being out in the barn with the animals trying to get them to calm down. The thunder and lightning had scared them and they wouldn't stop. Finally the storm subsided a bit and I made my way through the dark back to the house. When I opened the door I found my father soaked to the skin sitting at the kitchen table.

"Mary," he mumbled as he looked up at me and I knew that it was going to be a bad night. He usually didn't drink at home but I could see the bottle at his feet. He stood up leaning on the table for support and smiled at me. "I've missed you Mary."

I didn't say anything to him because I knew that it would just make him angrier. If I let him continue his fantasy he might be tired enough to fall asleep. If he got angry then I knew that he would just get riled up and violent.

"Let's get you to bed," I whispered and hung up my soaked shawl on the peg at the door. When I stepped forward to support him so he wouldn't fall over he pushed me away. I then realized that the water had soaked through my shawl and my dress and hair were both dripping wet. I looked up at him and with the speed of a sober man he reached out and grabbed a fist full of my hair.

"You're not Mary," he slurred as he looked at my blue eyes, his blue eyes. "Get away from me you temptress!" He said yanking my hair to the side to throw me away from him. I hit my hip on the table and stepped on his bottle which shattered it. I was grateful that I still had shoes on my feet or I would have glass in my feet. My father stumbled and fell to the floor with a thud. Then he tried to pull himself up on the chair but it toppled over. I knew that I was his only option and that if he got into bed he might sleep longer than he would on the floor.

Again I went to my father's side and slipped under his arm wrapping my arm around him to pull him upright. "You're so good to me Mary," He said and I grit my teeth. "You are so beautiful. That's why I love you so much." He said then stopped walking. I struggled under his weight as he leaned heavily against me to stay on his feet. "It is rude to ignore a compliment."

I glanced up at him knowing that I had made a mistake. "Thank you, my dear. You are very kind to say those things to me. Now, let's get you into bed so that your back won't hurt in the morning." We took another few steps. He paused then swayed to the side I went to grab him before he could fall and he wrapped both of his arms around me crushing me against him. The smell of the alcohol made my stomach turn as he held me tightly.

"I just love you so much."

"I love you too," I replied as I tried to peel myself out of his arms.

"You said it wrong."

He let me go and slapped me across the face with the back of his hand with enough force to make me stumble backwards and lose my balance. I fell against the table smacking the side of my face on the wood and landing in the pile of glass from his shattered bottle. The room spun from the force of the blow and from hitting the table.

"You said it wrong!" He screamed at me and lunged forward. Because he was so drunk his movements were awkward and I slipped away from him. I crawled on my hands and knees toward the door and scrambled out into the rain. I closed the door behind me knowing that with the latch on the door it would take a few tries for my father to make it out. He would most likely grow too frustrated and end up falling asleep on the kitchen floor before making it out. Blood was oozing from my arm and I knew that it would need to be stitched up. I held my arm close to my body and pulled myself up on the porch.

The yard swirled in front of me and I staggered forward knowing that I needed to get my arm stitched up. I hoped that I would be able to make it to the doctor's house before I passed out. It took nearly a half hour for me to get to his house. The storm had resumed and I was drenched as I pounded on his door with my good hand. There was a noise inside and the sound of footsteps. I saw a faint light which let me know that he had lit a match. The light grew as it was put into a lantern. I leaned against the door frame for support and his door cracked open as he pulled on a shirt over his bare chest.

"Lydia!" He gasped as I slumped forward. He caught me in his arms and I wrapped my arm around his chest. I sobbed against him and let him pull me into his house and sit me down at a chair. He brought over a lamp and started working on my arm removing the glass and cleaning the wound. He had wrapped a blanket around my shoulders and put a cup of warm tea in my hands. "I will need to sew it up," he explained as he looked at the gash. I nodded numbly because this wasn't the first time. He found his needle and thread then sat down in front of my again with our knees touching I grabbed the fabric at his shirtsleeve to keep myself still and he started sewing me up. There was a pinch and pull as the needle bit into my skin and the thread eased through.

Every now and then James would glance at my face. I could see the sadness in his eyes as he continued working. This was a regular thing for us every few months. I knew that he wanted to save me but there wasn't anything that he could do. My father wouldn't approve us a marriage between the two of us.

Once my arm was stitched he looked at the bump on my head from the table. I was exhausted and so he let me sleep on the little bed in the corner. He made some excuse about wanting to make sure that my head wound wasn't serious. I didn't care that it was improper to sleep in the home of a single man. I curled up in my damp clothes with the quilt wrapped around my shoulders and went to sleep.

"Did you come to check up on our patient?" James asked bringing me back to the present. I blinked a few times and smiled at him.

"He seems to be doing well. I would expect nothing less from your care."

James blushed at my praise then he stood up and walked over to me. Leading me by the elbow he steered me away from Peter. We walked out the front door and James closed it behind us. He crossed his arms over his chest and turned to face me.

"He seems to be doing much better now. I was thinking that you might be able to help me get him back on his feet."

"What do you need?"

"I think if he were to start moving around more and working he might be able to heal faster. If he doesn't over work himself it could be really helpful to him. I was thinking that he could come stay with you."

"I can discuss it with my father but you know how he is."

"I understand," James said with is hand on the door as he pushed it open allowing us to walk back inside with Peter. I looked at the man who I didn't really know. I knew that I had put him in this position and I felt responsible to help him get well again.

"I will talk it over with my father."

Chapter 10

(LYDIA)

I had to return home to my father a short time later. I knew that there was bread to bake and dinner to finish preparing. I hoped that the soup would stretch far enough to feet Ruben as well but I also knew that it would be rude to refuse him for dinner. The house came into view and I could see Ruben waiting for me at the back door of the barn with his arms crossed over his chest. He looked like he was ready to discipline a naughty child.

"Where were you?" He asked when I got closer. He reached out to take the reins of the horse as I jumped back down to the ground.

"I went into town."

"What for?"

"To get supplies for supper," I said gesturing to the saddle bag that had a few things that I hoped to add to the stew.

"You know that I could have gotten the supplies for you."

"I didn't want to bother you when you were speaking to my father," I said as I led the horse back to the stall where I would take off her saddle and rub her down. Ruben's hand shot out and grabbed my forearm. His fingers wrapped around tightly and when I tried to take my arm back from his grasp he tightened his grip. My fingers started to tingle. I knew that the only way to get him to let go was to let him talk. I turned to face him.

"You don't have to go into town."

I knew that he was trying to keep me at the farm. He wanted me to be able to do my work. I just needed to get away sometimes or I would go crazy.

"I am sorry," I said looking down at the floor of the barn. He reached forward and with a finger under my chin he lifted my face to look at him.

"All will be forgiven if you promise to not do it again without my permission."

"I won't go into town," I said feeling defeated. I knew that he just wanted to keep me safe. After everything that had happened I knew that staying at home wouldn't keep me safe.

"Now, let's go inside after you've finished with the horse and we can eat. I have an exciting announcement for you."

He let go of my arm and went to go lean against the door of the barn. I flexed my fingers and shook out my hand feeling the rush of blood return. I knew that Ruben just wanted me to be safe. He didn't want me to go places. I knew that he was worried about horses because one of his brothers had died after a horse riding accident.

I went to the stream to fill the buckets with fresh water for the horses and brought it back for them. Once my chores were done I returned to the house and Ruben sat down at the kitchen table while I finished with supper. The bread had risen and I put it in the oven. It was a small loaf and

I knew that it would cook quickly. I worked on making the stew stretch for supper. I added a few of the carrots that I had purchased to the stew that had been slowly cooking all day.

"What exciting news did you want to tell me?" I asked as I slid the last few ingredients into the cooking pot.

"I'll tell you when your father comes in for dinner," He said. I could smell the bread cooking and I knew that it would be ready in just a few minutes.

"I have something to tell you as well."

"What is it?" He asked with a smile.

"You'll also have to wait until my father comes in for dinner."

I cleaned up the table and straightened the kitchen so that we could eat together in a tidy room. I got the table set to perfection and sent Ruben outside to fetch my father. The men sat at the table and I served them their supper. The bread was cut into thick slabs and I set both of them a plate. Then I ladled the stew into their bowls. Adding the extra ingredients seemed to do the trick and there was enough for both of the men to have a large bowl. I got a bowl for myself and scraped the last of the stew into it.

My father said grace and we started eating. I wanted to ask what the surprise was but I knew that my father would tell me that I was being impatient and impolite. Ruben would tell me the news when the time was right. Eventually the bowls were emptied and the last bit of the stew was mopped up by the rest of the fresh bread. Ruben and my father wiped their hands while I cleared the table off and put the dishes in a tub of water to soak so that they would be easier to clean.

Ruben leaned back and sighed contentedly. He gave me an appreciative smile and I was happy to know that he still liked my cooking. I took my place at the table and waited. Ruben looked over at my father who nodded in agreement letting him know that it would be alright to proceed in telling me the news that he was so excited to share. Ruben leaned across the table to take my hand in his. I could see the excitement gleaming in his eyes as he started to tell me all about his exciting news.

"Lydia, your father and I have been talking. We have both agreed that you have reached the age in your life when it would be appropriate for you to find a husband. So, I have asked your father's permission to marry you and he has agreed. We shall be wed next week."

I looked at him dumbstruck.

I looked back and forth between him and my father. Both of them were smiling at me like it was the best thing in the world and that I should be excited that my future had been decided for me already. I opened my mouth and closed it again because I wasn't sure exactly what I was supposed to say or what I was supposed to do.

"Look at that, I've rendered her speechless," Ruben said looking proud of himself.

Slowly I withdrew my hand from his grasp and let it rest in my lap with the other one.

"Are you alright my dear?" Ruben asked and I could see the concern on his face.

"We're getting married?"

"Yes!"

"I never agreed to marry you," I said and I saw my father twitch. I was being horribly rude but I couldn't wrap my mind around what was happening. My father rose from his chair and placed his hands down on the table leaning forward so that he towered over me. I cowered down at the look on his face as he glared at me.

"You will agree to this, Lydia," He growled as he leaned down in my face. My hands curled into fists in my lap and I willed myself to remain seated. I knew that standing up and talking back would just make things worse. I looked across the table to see Ruben and he looked wounded. I scrambled for something to say that would smooth over this awkward situation.

"I have some news too," I said as I remembered what James and I had discussed earlier.

Neither of the men said anything to encourage me to continue with what I was saying so I just kept talking.

"I have befriended one of the Doctor's patients and I have agreed to let him stay here at the house."

"What?!" My father roared slapping his hands down on the table again making me jump at the sound of the loud crack.

"James says that in order for the man to heal he needs to be able to be working and doing things. I have agreed to let him stay with us in exchange for helping me out around the house and the land."

"He cannot stay here, I will not allow it," My father said. I glanced across the table at Ruben who stared at me with an open mouth as though I had grown a third eye.

"You have said before that I am too slow at completing my chores. If I had someone to help me I might be able to get them done quicker. He would be beneficial for us to have around."

"If I had a son I wouldn't have to worry about him being too weak to complete his duties."

"You had a son father! You drove him away and now he is gone!" I said as I stood up to face my father. I knew that it was dangerous to stand up to him but I also knew that he wouldn't hit me if Ruben was there. Of course Ruben knew about the abuse but my father wouldn't ever do something in front of Ruben.

I heard my father suck in a deep breath and I continued to do the same. I closed my eyes for a second to gather my courage then I opened them again to face him. "I have agreed to this and the man will be here in the morning."

I spun around and went outside into the night. I didn't bother to look behind me and neither man bothered to follow me. I marched out to the barn and climbed the ladder up into the small loft that was up in the top of the barn. I had spent many nights out there and I had a small bed already made up. The blankets smelled of hey and there was a soft pillow made out of rags. I sat down on the small bed and smiled to myself. I had defied my father and I had hired a man who was going to help out around the farm.

When Ruben came out into the barn calling my name I remained silent. I knew that my behavior was rather childish. I should have stood up and faced him. I also didn't know what to say. I knew that he wanted to kiss me goodnight but I feel like talking to him or anything else. He called my name a few more times then climbed up the ladder. I held perfectly still and I knew that he wouldn't be able to see me in the dark. He sighed then went back down the ladder. I could hear his soft footsteps as he walked across the hay covered floor. He let the barn door drop behind him and it closed with a loud bang which caused the horses to startle at the sound.

I sat on my bed thinking over the events from the night.

"We have both agreed that you have reached the age in your life when it would be appropriate for you to find a husband. So, I have asked your father's permission to marry you and he has agreed. We shall be wed next week."

I couldn't believe Ruben's words. He hadn't even asked me if I would like to marry him. I didn't expect my father to ask if I would like to spend the rest of my life with a man like Ruben. He was a decent man most of the time and he could make a decent husband.

I rolled over on the bed and huffed as I tried to get the image out of my mind. Me, clad in a white dress walking down an aisle. Ruben smiling at me at the end of the long line. I sighed and rolled over to the other side trying to get rid of the image. Ruben smiling at me holding our child in his arms. Ruben reaching out grabbing my arm too tightly or raising his hand to our child about to hit her. I sat up and ran a hand across my face. I knew that I couldn't marry Ruben. Marrying him would be just like marrying my father and I already knew that I didn't want to live a life like that.

I wanted to think of something else, anything else. Tomorrow would be a fresh day and a new start. I had a new friend coming to help out in the morning. I peeked over the edge of the loft at the horse down below. She would be excited to see her master again.

I smiled in the darkness.

I was sort of excited to see her master again too.

AUTHOR'S NOTE:

I am going to apologize in advance for the long delay that is coming your way. I am going in for a fairly extensive wrist surgery. Because of this, I won't be able to type for awhile. The next update might be in a few weeks or it might be in a few months. I just wanted to let you know that there will be more updates. I have an ending in mind for this story and I will be finishing it. I would also like to thank you in advance for patiently waiting for the next chapter. I hope to be able to post something soon!

Chapter 11

He followed the directions that the doctor had given him and soon the described farm house came into view as he walked down the road. Peter was grateful that the doctor had found something for him to do. The constant sitting all day was getting to his head and he felt like he was going crazy. The beautiful girl visiting was what brightened Peter's day. When James had suggested that he go out to work on her farm he had jumped at the opportunity.

Peter whistled as he walked with his hands in his pockets. The deep breaths were painful but it reminded him that he was alive. He sucked in a deeper breath and let out a tune as he walked. The door of the front house opened and a grouchy looking man walked out. He glared at Peter when Peter lifted his arm to wave at the man. His expression didn't change as he took a few steps forward an plopped down in an old rocking chair.

He didn't say anything as he pointed towards the barn. Peter didn't need to be told twice. He spun on his heel and went in the direction of the weathered looking structure. When he opened the door he was delighted to see his horse in a stall and looking taken care of.

"How are you doing pretty girl?" He asked.

"Excuse me?"

Peter jumped to see the girl descending the ladder to his left. He remembered her name was Lydia.

"I was talking to my horse," He said and his cheeks colored instantly. "Not
that you're not a pretty girl too I just didn't want you to think I was being
too forward..." he trailed off and felt his cheeks get even warmer. He was
sure he was bright red. Lydia looked at him and laughed at his expression.
She had a few pieces of straw stuck in her hair and it was evident from
her wrinkled clothes from the previous day that she had slept in the barn.
Peter wondered why she had spent the night in the loft. From her father's
disgruntled expression it was clear that he was excited about having a visitor
for a while. Peter wondered if he was the reason that she had slept outside
and he immediately felt guilty. "Is it alright that I am here?"

Lydia paused and looked at him with wide eyes as though she were trying
to come up with something to say. Peter wondered if she was going to make
something up about him staying to make him feel better about it.

"Your father didn't look very happy to see me when I walked into the yard
a few minutes ago."

"My father is rarely happy to see anyone other than the bartender in town.
It isn't your fault that he behaves like a child. This is my house too and you
are welcome to stay with us."

After her little speech she walked away from him and grabbed a bucket
that was hanging from a hook on the wall of the barn. Even though it was
empty Peter stepped forward to take it from her. She looked back in shock
and tightened her grip on the handle of the bucket.

"Allow me," Peter said as he tugged the bucket free from her hand. Her perfect composure disappeared as her mouth dropped open. Slowly her fingers released one by one and Peter took the empty bucket from her. He retrieved the other one off of the hook and together they made their way to the back of the barn. He rushed ahead of her and held the barn door open for her with the two buckets swinging at his side in one hand. Again she stared at him in shock as she walked out the door that he held.

"Thank you," She whispered and he nodded to accept the thanks. "Are you going to allow me to do anything?" She asked.

"I will allow you to show me the way to the stream."

<<<><><>>>

(LYDIA)

"You really shouldn't overwork yourself on your first day back."

"Overwork myself?" Peter said then gestured to the bandage around his chest that was under his shirt. "Over this little scratch? I've cut myself worse than this when I was shaving. This is nothing," He said as he stooped down to fill the bucket with water from the stream. I could tell from the look on his face that it was painful but as quick as the expression appeared it was gone. He scooped up the water and then reached for the other bucket that was sitting on the ground next to him. Again he bent over to fill the bucket with water.

"Let me help you with those," I said once both of the buckets were full. He was quicker than I was and he grabbed both of the handles on the buckets and stood up. I stared at him in shock again. I could barely manage to hold one of the buckets on my own. He didn't show any sign of strain as he walked ahead of me back towards the barn. "You won't let me carry even one of them?" I asked as I hurried to catch up with his long legged stride.

"If I carry only one at a time I will have to walk lopsided. You wouldn't want that would you? I might reopen my stitches."

"You're ridiculous," I said and he set the buckets down to spin around and look at me. I immediately stepped back and felt myself shrink. He was much larger than my father. I could imagine what a smack from him would feel like. Again I had let my tongue run away without me. "I'm sorry," I whimpered and his expression softened. It was then that I realized that he had been smiling. He hadn't been angry about my comment. He had noticed that I had shrunk away from him and he had a look of concern on his face.

"It's alright. I've been called many things that are worse than being called ridiculous."

I didn't want to see the look on his face as he tried to figure out my reaction. I walked in front of him. "The barn is this way," I said softly as I took the lead. I held the door for him as he walked through with the buckets. He thanked me and continued to fill up the troughs. They still needed a few trips to be completely full. There was no use in the both of us going together and me standing there useless so I let him go back by himself.

"What if I fall and reopen my stitches?" He teased.

"Then scream really loud and I might send someone to come find you."

He tipped his head back and laughed loudly as he walked out the back door of the barn. I started filling the feed buckets and putting them out for the horses. Then I set to work cleaning out the stalls after I let the horses outside the barn to walk around and stretch their legs. I started cleaning with the rake as Peter walked back through the door and dumped the buckets in the troughs.

"What are you doing?" He asked.

"I'm cleaning the stalls."

"Here," He said as he stepped forward and took the rake from my hand. "How about I finish this and you could get something started for breakfast."

I almost didn't know what to do as he took the rake from me and started cleaning. This was always mine and my mother's job when I was younger. As I got older and my mother passed away it had become my job. My father never offered to help. I looked outside at the sky and I knew that it was still early.

"Alright," I said as I left him to do his work. I went to gather up the eggs from the coop. There were several large brown eggs and I praised my girls for their excellent work. They clucked their replies as I dropped some feed down for them and went inside the house to get started on some breakfast for my father and our guest. I cracked the eggs into a pan and set to work making some batter for a few pancakes. While it wouldn't be much it would be something special to thank our guest for his help.

The eggs sizzled and the pancakes browned as I flipped them and stirred everything. There was the sound of boots on the porch and I heard the quiet sounds of a conversation. The creaking of my father's rocking chair continued and I knew that he would be ignoring Peter and staring off into space with a blank look on his face. The front door opened and Peter walked in carrying a bucket of milk from the cow..

"Is he alright?" He asked gesturing to the front porch as he set the milk on the table.

"He is perfectly fine. He just acts like a spoiled child because he can get away with it," I said softly as Peter walked over to the pitcher and basin and cleaned himself up a bit before breakfast. He wiped his hands on the towel and leaned over to look into the pan to see what was for breakfast.

"That smells delicious."

"Thank you," I replied as I felt my face heat up in embarrassment. My cooking was rarely complimented. It was nice to have something as simple as breakfast recognized. The creaking of the rocking chair paused on the front porch and I knew that my father was getting up. I rushed to get the table set so that everything would be perfect for when he walked in.

The front door opened and my father dropped down on one of the kitchen chairs. I hoped and prayed that he would behave for our guest as I placed a steaming plate in front of him. He said nothing as he grabbed a fork and started digging in. I served Peter a plate too and he thanked me.

Our new guest was puzzling. I hadn't ever met someone who said thank you all the time and gave me compliments. It put me on edge because it was so strange. Peter waited for me to get my own plate and sit down. Once I had my fork in my hand he reached for his fork. I cut the pancake and speared a piece bringing it up to my mouth. After I had started eating, Peter started eating.

Yet again I was puzzled by his behavior and I decided that I still had many things to learn about this new house guest of ours. Once breakfast was finished my father pushed away from the table and went outside plopping down in his rocking chair just like usual. The creaking resumed. I stood up and reached for my father's discarded plate. Peter reached over and took both my plate and my father's plates from my hands and went to go clean them.

"What are you doing?" I stammered as he took them over to the sink that still had last nights dishes soaking in them in cold water.

"I am washing the dishes?" He said and he set the dishes in the sink. "Is that alright?" He asked turning to face me where I was frozen in the middle of the kitchen.

"Why?"

"Where I come from, if the woman does the cooking the men will do the dishes. It isn't fair that you do all of the work."

With that simple explanation he continued with the dishes. The cold water from the previous night was dumped out the back door and replaced with hot water. I got a towel and dried the dishes after he washed them.

The day continued like that as we worked to get all of the chores completed. All day long I was puzzled by his strange behavior. When it was beginning to get dark we made our way back into the barn to return our tools. Peter had helped me all day and I could tell that it had an effect on him. He leaned against one of the stalls with his hand against his chest.

"Peter?" I asked and he didn't move. "Are you alright?"

"I'm fine," he said softly.

"Let me see."

He didn't move his hand away from his chest until I placed my hand on his and pushed it gently away. He looked pale as I lifted his shirt up to see the bandage. It was soaked through with blood and sweat.

"Why didn't you tell me?!" I gasped as I pulled his shirt off and started examining the wound.

"You would have made me stop."

"Of course I would have made you stop!"

I pulled on the bandage unwrapping it from around his chest. I didn't want to unwrap it all the way because I was afraid of what I would find underneath. I grit my teeth and pulled it the rest of the way. Peter hissed as it stuck in the blood and then pulled free. The stitches had opened up a bit and they were bleeding. I knew that James would say that I had overworked him but he hadn't given me any sign that he needed to rest.

"We need to get you into town to see the doctor."

Peter protested as I got him onto his horse and I climbed up with him. He had lost a lot of blood and it was clear that he was exhausted. We made our way into town as quickly as I dared. Peter protested the entire time. Once we were outside of the doctor's house I pulled the horse to a stop and dropped down to the ground. Peter eased off of the horse and wrapped his arm around me.

"Let's get you inside," I wheezed as he leaned heavily on me. I got him up the stairs and on the porch before I could knock he passed out falling on me. I lost my balance and fell to the ground with Peter on top of me.

"Lydia?" I heard a familiar voice call as I struggled to get out from underneath Peter. Ruben stood in the middle of the street looking at us in our awkward position on the side of the doctor's house.

I detangled myself from Peter and rolled out from underneath him.

"Did he force himself on you?!" Ruben gasped.

"What?"

"He assaulted you!" Ruben said getting louder and louder. People were walking out on their porches listening to the spectacle. "He took advantage of you!!"

I hurried to Peter's side and tried to roll him over.

"I can't believe that you can force yourself to touch him!" Ruben hissed. "After what he did to you!"

"He didn't do anything to me Ruben, you know that."

"I only know what I saw. I saw him force himself on you!" He leaned into my face. "You know what the law calls for," He whispered into my ear. Ruben took a step back and extended his arms out at his sides as people gathered around us.

"It is my duty to protect this woman as my betrothed! I saw this man force himself on her!!" The people gasped at Ruben's accusations and they looked at me as my mind raced. "You know what the law calls for and I will see that it is upheld!" The people cheered their approval.

"Ruben you can't do this! You know nothing happened!"

"It's good of you to try to protect him even after what he did to you," He said to me. Again he extended his arms at his sides. "It is my duty to see that he is hanged for his crimes against this woman!"

A cheer erupted from all of the people around us.

AUTHOR'S NOTE:

I tried my best to get one last chapter for you before my surgery. Have a good one my friends! I will be back in a few weeks. (Fingers crossed)

Chapter 12

(RUBEN)

Ruben watched as Lydia rode into the yard. He crossed his arms over his chest as he watched her avoid his gaze.

"Where were you?" He demanded as she came closer. Ruben took a few steps towards her as he waited for a reply that would explain her disappearance. Ruben reached out to take the reins of her horse so she couldn't ride away from him. Lydia dropped down to the ground looking pleased with herself.

"I went into town," she said as she took the reins from him.

"What for?"

She gestured to the bulging saddle bags that were dangling off of the horse saddle. "To get supplies for supper."

Ruben felt his temper flare up. She knew that he hated it when she went into town by herself. There was no reason for her to go in all alone. Her place was in the home.

"You know that I could have gotten the supplies for you."

"I didn't want to bother you when you were speaking to my father," she took the horse into the barn. Ruben felt an excited shiver run through him at the mention of his conversation with her father.

Lydia turned her back on him as she unbuckled the saddle. His excitement disappeared as she turned her back to him. Ruben hated it when she turned away from him when he was talking to her. His arm shot out and grabbed her tightly. When she tried to pull free he tightened his grip. Ruben wondered what had gotten into her. Something must have happened to her while she was in town. He tightened his grip.

"You don't have to go into town," Ruben growled feeling his free hand twitch. He held it down at his side because he didn't want to hit her. He had to keep enough control of himself so that he didn't hurt her. At least not now.

"I am sorry," She said sounding sincere and he let his fingers loosen one by one off of her arm. He lifter her chin forcing her to look him in the eye.

"All will be forgiven if you promise to not do it again without my permission."

"I won't go into town," she said and he saw her shoulders slump slightly.

"Now, let's go inside after you have finished with the horse and we can eat. I have an exciting announcement for you."

Ruben felt the excitement bubbling up in him again. He had spoken to Lydia's father and he had granted his request of marriage. He knew that Lydia would be as excited as he was. The joining of their families would be beneficial for everyone. Lydia needed a strong man to look after her and keep her in line. She tended to have a rebellious streak that could get her into trouble. What she needed was a firm hand to make sure that she stayed in line. Ruben would also benefit from the union. He would have someone to work with him. He would also get a wife and a mother for all of the children that he would have. He would be the head of the household, of course, and she would be there to take care of him.

Ruben could already imagine all of the jealous glances and glares from the other men in town. It was no secret that Lydia was beautiful. Once she had some training and learned to behave herself she would be absolutely perfect. Ruben could already picture her on his arm as they strolled through the town. Ruben let his thoughts run as Lydia finished up with her chores.

Once she was finished he followed her into the house and sat down at the table.

"What exciting news did you want to tell me?"

"I'll tell you when your father comes in for dinner."

"I have something to tell you as well."

"What is it?"

"You'll also have to wait until my father comes in for dinner."

After dinner was made and the table was set Ruben went out front to tell Lydia's father that it was time to eat. The men sat down and waited as Lydia cut the bread and scooped soup into bowls. They ate quickly and Ruben was trying to figure out how to tell her his news. After Lydia had the table cleared after their meal Ruben offered her his most dazzling smile. She gave him a small smile in return then she finally sat down at the table. Ruben could couldn't contain himself any longer so her reached across the table to take Lydia's hand in his.

"Lydia, your father and I have been talking. We have both agreed that you have reached the age in your life when it would be appropriate for you to find a husband. So, I have asked your father's permission to marry you and he has agreed. We shall be wed next week." The words tumbled out of his mouth in an excited rush and he could tell from her expression that she was as equally excited as he was. She looked back and forth between him and her father and he knew that she was trying to come up with a way to thank him for the offer of her hand.

Her mouth opened and closed.

"Look at that, I've rendered her speechless," Ruben said. Lydia eased her hand from his and let it fall into her lap. "Are you alright my dear?"

"We're getting married?"

She asked and Ruben couldn't believe how slow she was being. "Yes!" he exclaimed.

"I never agreed to marry you."

"You will agree to this, Lydia!" Her father said as he stood up rising up from his chair.

"I have some news too," she said looking flustered. "I have befriended one of the Doctor's patients, and I have agreed to let him stay here at the house."

"What?!" Her father roared slapping his hands down on the table again and Ruben saw Lydia jump from the loud crack.

"James says that in order for the man to heal he needs to be able to be working and doing things. I have agreed to let him stay with us in exchange for helping me out around the house and the land."

"He cannot stay here, I will not allow it," Her father said and Ruben couldn't agree more. He could only imagine what would happen if his intended were to spend time with a man around the house.

"You have said before that I am too slow at completing my chores. If I had someone to help me I might be able to get them done quicker. He would be beneficial for us to have around."

"If I had a son I wouldn't have to worry about him being too weak to complete his duties."

"You had a son father! You drove him away and now he is gone!" Lydia said as she stood up to face her father. "I have agreed to this and the man will be here in the morning."

Lydia stormed outside and Ruben looked at her father in shock. He hadn't ever seen behavior like that from her before. It was just more evidence that she needed to be settled down with a husband who had a strong hand. "I'll go out and find where she has run off too," Ruben volunteered standing up from the table.

He walked out into the yard calling her name. When she didn't reply he climbed up on his horse and rode out into the night.

The next day Ruben stayed away from Lydia's house. part of him wanted to go over and see what she was doing with her new hired hand. He battled with himself trying to make up his mind. She had to know that he was the best possible match for her. He kept telling himself this throughout the day. She would be loyal to him because they were engaged. He also knew that her father would keep an eye on her and any of her inappropriate behavior would be stopped immediately.

He sighed and tried to push Lydia out of his thoughts. He shoved a hand through his hair and kicked at a pebble with his toe. He needed something to take his mind off of her. Ruben got his horse ready and set off in the direction of the town. He knew the perfect place to help him get his mind off of his troubles, even if it was only for a few hours.

He tied his horse up out front to a well used post. There were already several other horses tied up. Ruben walked in through the familiar doors and let his eyes adjust to the dark room that was lit by candles. Only a small amount of light drifted in through the tiny windows that were around the room. Later on in the evening the windows wouldn't provide enough light and there would be a roaring fire burning. Ruben found a place to sit and thought about what he would have. After exchanging the payment he had a strong drink in his hands. He took a drink of the liquid that burned his throat and tickled his nose.

Ruben lost track of time. He didn't notice the lengthening shadows from the windows. He ignored the growl of his stomach. Only when the large fire was lit did he realize that he had spent the entire day trying to get Lydia off of his mind. His pockets were considerably lighter as he made his way outside. The slap of the cold night air helped to wake him up and clear the fog from his mind a bit. Ruben took a deep breath of the fresh air and shook his head back and forth. He found his horse and was about to start untying it when he noticed a commotion behind him. When he turned around he saw Lydia on a horse rushing to the doctor's house.

When Ruben realized that she wasn't alone on the horse he made his way over to her on his wobbly legs. He watched as she jumped down from the horse then helped down the man who was with her. She pulled one of his arms around her shoulder and wrapping her other arm around his waist to support him then they started walking. The man was leaning on her and Ruben could see that she was struggling under his weight. Ruben felt that jealous spark again and watched as she got the two of them up the stairs. She paused in front of the door unable to get the door open without letting the man go. She was about to knock with her foot against the door when the man who was leaning on her staggered.

Ruben rushed to her side as she was pinned on the porch. "Lydia?" He called to her as she tried to roll out from underneath the large body that was holding her down. She managed to slide out from underneath him and she crouched down at his side. Ruben's jealous spark was replaced by a red hot jealous rage.

"Did he force himself on you?"

"What?" Lydia gasped in horror finally turning around to face Ruben in the middle of the road.

"He assaulted you!" Ruben said getting louder and louder. By now people were walking out of their houses and onto their porches as they watched and listened to the spectacle that was in front of them. "He took advantage of you!"

Lydia turned back to get to the man's side as she tried to get him rolled over.

"I can't believe that you can force yourself to touch him!" Ruben hissed. "After what he did to you!"

"He didn't do anything to me Ruben, you know that!"

Ruben knew what he had seen but he also knew what his heart was telling him. He could see the way that she touched him as she tried to get him to open his eyes and look at her. Ruben looked up to see James open the door because of the commotion. He immediately crouched down next to Lydia and the man on the ground. Ruben felt the bubble of jealousy grow inside of him. The doctor was yet another man who was trying to steal Lydia away from him. While he couldn't do anything about the doctor right now he could do something about Lydia's new hired hand.

"I only know what I saw!" Ruben bellowed as he walked over towards her. "I saw him force himself on you!" Ruben leaned down to whisper in her ear. "You know what the law calls for."

Ruben stood upright and extended his arms at his sides. His gaze swept over the audience that had gathered to make sure that he had everyone's attention.

"It is my duty to protect this woman as my betrothed! I saw this man force himself on her!" Ruben paused to let that sink in. There were a few audible gasps as the people realized what was going on. "You know what the law calls for and I will see that it is upheld!"

"Ruben you can't do this! You know nothing happened!" Lydia looked desperate as she tried to protect a stranger that she barely knew.

"It's good of you to try to protect him even after what he did to you. It is my duty to see that he is hanged for his crimes against this woman!"

A cheer erupted from all of the people that had gathered around. They raised their arms up high in the air and stepped forward inching towards Lydia and the man who now had his eyes open and was sitting up with the help of James and Lydia.

Ruben saw James and Lydia share a glance. Ruben reminded himself that he was the one who was engaged to Lydia. The doctor wouldn't be able to look at her much longer without facing a major consequence. The people got closer to Lydia and James stood up with his arms raised up in front of him.

"This man is my patient and I will see that he gets a fair trial. First, I will tend to his injuries." The doctor looked back at Lydia and offered her a sympathetic smile. There wasn't anything that he could do to prevent the trial from happening. "The trial will be in two days from now to decide his fate!"

Chapter 13

- -

(LYDIA)

"What were you thinking?!" I demanded once I was alone with James and Peter. "A trial won't make any difference! The entire town is out there already calling for his blood."

"I don't know," James said as he shoved his hands through his hair and leaned his arms on his knees. "I thought that it might give us some time to get all of this figured out. Hopefully we can come up with a solution."

"It won't make any difference you heard the people out there, they have already made up their minds the want to see him hang."

James didn't listen to me. Instead he went back to the unconscious Peter's wounds. I pushed his hands away and put my hands on my hips glaring at him.

"What are you doing?!" I demanded.

"What does it look like? I'm attending to his wounds."

"It would be cruel to heal him just so that he can be healthy enough to die. It would be far better to let him bleed out right here and now. Let him have some dignity." I said as I thought of the horrible executions that I had seen in the past. They were always a large spectacle in town and many of the people loved to attend. It was a horrible morbid tradition that people always turn out when there was a public execution. My father had always insisted that we go to them. My mother would plead with him to let us stay home but he would say that we should go together as a family like all of the other towns people. My father would lift me up on to his shoulders and hold my mother close at his side forcing us to watch. We weren't allowed to close our eyes or cover our ears to block out the sounds. The hangings from my childhood always haunted me. I could imagine the crunching bones as necks were suddenly broken with a short drop and a sudden stop.

And those were the lucky ones.

I had seen a few hangings where the rope took several long minutes to be effective all the while the writhing body hung suspended. Legs kicking looking for a foot hold to end their torment as they slowly suffocated. They would do anything for just one more fresh breath of air. When their efforts would prove pointless they would hang with their heads lolled back, eyes bulging, and tongue swollen. Their bowels would release. A sword would be thrust through their chests to make sure that they were really dead. I had always thought that the sword should have been used instead of the rope. A quick wound to the heart was quicker and seemed better than the rope. I looked at Peter's face and I couldn't imagine wishing that fate on anyone.

"Something tells me that his life isn't over yet," James whispered as he set to work.

<<<><><>>>

(LYDIA)

I stared at the people around me. Many of them I had known for years. While they had not ever been my friends I didn't expect them to turn on me so quickly. They looked at me as though they couldn't believe that I would dare to defend the man who had supposedly attacked me. I constantly proclaimed Peter's innocence while the people continually condemned him.

I searched Eliza's face out in the crowd and she offered me a friendly smile. I wondered what she thought of this spectacle. Surely she would be the only person who believed me when I said that Peter hadn't done anything wrong. James had proclaimed Peter healthy enough to kill and was sitting near Eliza. Out of the entire town they were the only two people who weren't calling for Peter to hang. I looked straight ahead to Peter who was sitting at the front of the group all alone. His hands were bound in front of him to prevent his stitches from ripping open again. Ruben would have considered it a tragedy if he were to bleed out and we had to start this entire thing over.

I wondered if Peter regretted coming here. I wondered if he regretted saving me in the very beginning. His life would have been better if he had just let Orvil kill me. I wanted to ask him but I knew that he wouldn't ever admit it. Ruben was pacing back and forth behind Peter. Every now and then he would look up at me and smile. I wasn't sure if he was smiling to assure me that everything was going to be alright or if he was just smiling to let me know that he had won.

My father staggered into the gathering and I knew that he had been drinking. He wouldn't miss the opportunity to get a drink if he had made the trip all the way into town. I frowned as he dropped into a chair nearly missing the seat. I knew what would be waiting for me at home after this horrid day ended.

Ruben's father wobbled down and dropped down next to my father. The two of them burst out laughing as they tried to steady each other. The people around them wrinkled their noses in disgust and I realized that it didn't matter what I said. I would still be seen as the daughter of the town drunk. I would always be viewed as the dirty little girl who was covered in bruises. I would be seen as the poor little girl whose mother died after living under the thumb of a cruel man. I pulled my eyes away from my father as Ruben cleared his throat loudly to get the attention of all of the people who were there to watch the hanging.

The crowd was suddenly quiet and I turned around to look at them. There were many people seated behind me. It was sad that it took the public death of someone to get everyone out of their houses. I could see the fathers standing at the back of the crowd because there weren't enough chairs for everyone to sit down. The fathers stood with their children hoisted up on their shoulders for a better view. Buckets had been overturned to use as stools for people to see over the crowds. It turned my stomach to see all of the expectant faces that were waiting for the results of the trial. I knew that Peter would be found guilty. I would forever be viewed as a tainted woman and Ruben would be seen as a hero if he still agreed to marry me.

"All of you know why you have been gathered here today!" Ruben yelled so that all of the people could hear him. "One of our own was attacked as she attempted to take a sick man to the house of our good doctor. Today her attacker will be dealt with and he won't ever hurt another young woman again. If he is found guilty." Ruben added hastily at the end.

He had already made up his mind what would happen to Peter. This trial was pointless. His fate had already been decided. We were just prolonging the inevitable. Ruben knew it and I knew it too. He was laughing at my attempt to save Peter. As far as the town was concerned Peter was guilty. I wracked my brain trying to come up with a solution that would get Peter out of this predicament.

Ruben continued on with all of his evidence that proved Peter was an awful person and deserved to die this horrible death. I didn't hear half of the things that he said because I was trying to come up with something of my own to say in his defense.

"We have many laws that are important to be upheld or we wouldn't have any order." Ruben continued but I was focused on one word 'laws'. All of a sudden it made perfect sense what I was supposed to do to get Peter out of all of this. Ruben continued on with his account of what had happened and how it was important for us to protect each other. Ruben explained that he was only doing this to make sure that I was protected. He said that it was his duty to see that swift justice was delivered to anyone who dared hurt me.

There were cheers from the crowd as Ruben finished talking. "Is there anything else that you would like to add, dearest?"

"Yes," I said in a quiet whisper. I gathered up my courage as I stood and walked to stand next to Peter where he sat. I tried to give him a confident smile. The crowd kept talking as I tried to get their attention. I yelled for them to silence but nothing happened. Peter lifted his bound hands and put two fingers in his mouth to let out a shrill whistle. "Thank you," I said to him as I faced the now silent crowd.

"I have something that I would like to say," I said. The mumble of voices started again. There were calls for the noose and to get on with it already. I searched the faces of the crowd for Eliza and she gave me an encouraging smile and nodded at me to let me know that she was listening to me.

"I have something to say!" I screamed at the top of my lungs with a volume that even surprised me. The voices were silenced immediately. "It looks like you have already found this man guilty!" An undeniable cry of guilty rose up and I knew precisely what I had to do. I sucked in a deep breath before I continued as I prayed that Peter would forgive me.

"It is our law that when someone is accused of this horrible crime there are two solutions!" I yelled and Ruben looked at me with wide eyes as though he were daring me to continue. He looked shocked but most of all he looked angry. I made eye contact with Peter wondering if he knew what was going on. I wondered if he would ever forgive me for what I was about to do. I pulled my eyes away from him and I addressed the crowd. I was happy to see James with a huge smile plastered on his face. I now knew why he had insisted on the trial. He had thought of something and was hoping that I would catch on.

"My friends and neighbors!" I yelled so that I could be heard and so that nobody would be able to deny my decision. "By our law there are two solutions when someone is accused of this deplorable crime. Death!" I yelled and the people cheered. I waited for them to quiet down. "Or marriage!" There was a gasp as the people realized what I was saying. "You have found this man in front of you guilty. As a solution to his crime that was committed I choose marriage!" The people gasped and I saw my father's eyes bulge as my decision finally sunk in. He slapped his knees and stood up with his hands clenching into fists. I could see the anger in his eyes as he wobbled in his drunkenness trying to figure out how to get to me.

"What are you doing?!" Peter hissed at me.

"You saved my life once, let me save yours," I whispered to him. I turned back to the crowd that was full of disbelief. "Good doctor!" I yelled above the many voices, "If you would be willing I would like for you to marry us!"

James stood up from his seat and made his way forward. "I was hoping that you would catch on," he said as he took my hand.

"Why didn't you tell me this days ago?"

"I thought it would be better if you worked it out for yourself."

"What if I hadn't?"

He shrugged and started to cut the rope that was around Peter's hands. "I just knew that you would get it, eventually."

"You can't do this!" My father roared and James and Peter stepped in front of me.

"Do you deny the law?" James asked. "Do you deny the law that kept you shielded all those years as you beat your wife and daughter? Your daughter is a grown woman and she has the right to make decisions for herself without anyone interfering, according to the law. Unless you deny it?"

My father grumbled and unclenched his fists. He took one last hateful look at me then spat on the ground at our feet. He turned his back on us and walked back into the crowd. Ruben followed him without bothering to look back over his shoulder.

"If neither of you have any objections let's get on with it and make sure that this swift justice is delivered," James said mocking Ruben's words from earlier.

I shook my head. Peter looked at me for a while and I wondered what he was thinking. He then shook his head as well.

"Then, let's begin."

Author's Note:

Two updates in one day! What is this?!

I just got put in a cast and it is extremely difficult to type with so I am half as fast because I have half as many hands to type with. I felt guilty for slacking so I tried my best to get a couple updates for you to reward your patience. I am still really slow so I ask you to bear with me as I update slowly. Thank you for your prayers I am sure that they helped with my speedy recovery. As always, thank you for reading!

Chapter 14

(LYDIA)

James placed my hand in Peter's as he led us forward. We now stood a bit away from the tall gallows and I smiled at the turn of events. The crowd behind us had started dispersing and there were few people that remained. I found it odd that a public execution would get more attendance than a wedding. Eliza was one of the people remaining and she walked forward to stand at my side. My father had marched away and now there wasn't anyone to give me away. Eliza stood beside me to act as a stand in and give me to Peter in marriage.

"What a turn of events!" James commented excitedly. I glanced over at Peter and he was facing forward not looking at me. I started to worry. In the few short days that I had known Peter he had been open and carefree. His silence worried me. We were still holding hands and I took that as a good sign. If he had been repulsed by me he would have let my hand go.

"I promise," Peter whispered and it was then that I realized that James had begun. I had nearly missed everything because of my daydreaming. I glanced at their faces and realized that they were waiting for me to accept as well.

"I promise," I said quickly realizing that I had just promised to honor and obey a man that I barely knew. James took our free hands and placed them together so now I was holding both of Peter's hands. His large hands wrapped around mine making them feel small and powerless.

"I pronounce you husband and wife," James said then he took a step back. I looked up to search Peter's eyes but he was looking over my left shoulder. His eyes flickered down to mine and he swooped down to press his lips against mine. Then he was gone. The kiss was short and sweet and nothing like the kisses from Ruben. I felt more in the quick peck from Peter than from all of the kisses from Ruben combined. I was surprised at the quickening of my heart and the heat that was spreading across my cheeks. Peter released me to turn and talk with James. I turned around to see what Peter had been looking at over my shoulder. All that I saw was Ruben's retreating form.

It had all been for him.

A quick kiss as a show of possession. Peter had claimed me with his kiss letting Ruben know that he couldn't get to me anymore. I was grateful to be out of his reach even if it meant that I belonged to Peter now. I had promised to belong to Peter.

Eliza walked over and took my hands in hers. Feeling the warmth of her fingers made me realize just how cold my own hands were. She had a smile on her face and it reached all the way up into her eyes.

"That was a brave thing that you did," she said.

"I hope it was the right thing to do," I glanced at Peter and wondered what I had gotten myself into. I didn't even know the man.

"It was the right thing to do. He is rather handsome!" She whispered excitedly but by the changed in Peter's posture I knew that he had heard her. He had been listening in on our conversation. "What are you going to do now?"

"I don't know, I haven't thought that far ahead."

"You're welcome to come and stay at my house for a few days. I will be leaving to go visit a friend and you would be able to have the place to yourselves."

"That's very kind of you," I replied as I tried to think of a polite way to refuse her offer. I didn't really want to be alone with Peter but I also didn't want to be at my house with him and my father. I couldn't think more than two minutes ahead.

"Excellent! It is settled then."

I heard Peter clear his throat and I knew that it was time for us to go. He came to stand at my side and he nodded at Eliza. Her wrinkled cheeks turned red. Her mouth opened and then closed like she was trying to think of something to say. She was like a little school girl standing in front of her first crush.

"We should be going," Peter said taking my elbow.

"Eliza has offered for us to stay in her house while she is away for a few days visiting one of her friends."

"Thank you for your kindness."

"I have known this dear girl for most of her life. Anything that I can do to help the two of you is my pleasure."

"We will go collect Lydia's things and then we will be over shortly. Do you need any help packing your things?" Peter asked

"No, I'll be alright. I'll be leaving from here and the house will be empty by the time that you get there."

Peter and I walked in silence all the way to my farm. I didn't know what to say to him and he didn't seem like he wanted to talk. He walked my my side and every now and then our hand would brush. Each time he would angle his hand away from mine until finally he tucked both of his hands into his pocket. I turned down the path that would take us home and quickened my pace. When I saw my father sitting in his rocking chair on the porch I slowed.

I had expected him to still be in town with his friends drinking the day away. Instead he was in his usual spot looking drunker than usual. I didn't want to have to deal with this today. I didn't want Peter to see what my father was really like. I went slowly through the yard and Peter remained at my side.

"There she is!" My father slurred and stood up from his chair on wobbly legs. "Everyone bow down it's the town slut." I felt Peter flinch next to me at my father's harsh words.

"Lydia, why don't you go inside and gather your things while I speak to your father."

"She has nothing in there!" My father took a step on his weak legs and had to use the porch railing to keep himself upright.

"Go," Peter said to me and I inched past my father. I expected him to lunge at me but he couldn't even see straight with his bloodshot eyes. Even if he had lunged at me I would have been able to dodge him. I grasped the familiar door handle and shoved the door open with my shoulder. It was dark inside the house and I realized that the curtains had been drawn. After being out in the bright sunlight it took a moment for my eyes to adjust. I didn't see the dark figure approach me until he was just a few inches away.

"How could you do that to me? To us?"

I recognized Ruben's voice. I was about to open the door and call out for Peter but Ruben put his hand over my mouth and backed me up against the wall. I could smell the alcohol on his breath and feel the heat from his body as he pressed up against me.

"I would have been there for you. I would have provided for your every need. I would have been the perfect Master for you." He leaned down to press his face against my neck. His hot breath washed over me as he exhaled. "You threw it all away." He pushed my hair behind my ears studying my face. "I don't know what I ever saw in you."

I pushed with my arms and finally got him off of me. I darted into my small room and pushed a chair up against the door. I saw the handle jiggle and I knew that Ruben was trying to get in. The door shuddered as he shoved his shoulder against it. Seeing the door shake brought back memories from when I was a child. I would hide in my room underneath my bed with the chair wedged against the door. My father would throw himself against it trying to get the door open. Sometimes he was successful and would barge into the room. His large hands would reach under my bed grabbing me by whatever he could get a hold of. Other times he would give up and sink down against the door trapping me inside. His loud snores would keep me company for most of the night as I was kept awake too terrified to sleep.

There was a loud bang as Ruben threw himself against the door. I saw the chair legs slide an inch and I knew that the chair wouldn't hold forever. I grabbed a sack that I had used in the past to carry laundry in from the stream after it had been washed. I quickly loaded my few possessions into it. A dress from my mother that was worn and faded. One of her hair combs that had survived. The other had been smashed to pieces. I dropped in the apron that Eliza had made for me and tied the sack shut. It held everything that I owned in the world. I slung the bag over my shoulder and waited for Ruben to throw himself against the door one more time. I pressed an ear against the wood and listened for any sound that would tell me where Ruben was. All that I could hear was the sound of my father and Peter arguing out on the porch.

"She will be coming with me and you won't ever see her again!" I heard Peter roar and the front door was opened forcibly. "Lydia!" He called and I could hear the anger in his voice. It made me shiver. I knew what happened when men got angry. The doorknob jiggled and he called out again. I pulled the chair away from the door and opened it to face him. "Do you have your things?" He asked and I glanced at the bag that was strung over my shoulder. He looked at it then back at me. "Is that everything?" He asked and I nodded. "Then let's go." He reached down to take my hand in his and practically pulled me out of the house. We didn't slow to say goodbye to my father. Instead we marched right past him. I didn't look back to see my home or to see where Ruben was hiding. I could feel their eyes on me as we walked to the barn.

"Your father decided to give us this horse as a wedding gift. Wasn't that kind of him?" Peter had the animal saddled up and ready to go in moments. He grabbed me around the waist and tossed me up into the saddle. Then he led the horse out of the barn and climbed up behind me. His thighs pressed against mine as I wound my hands into the horse's mane to stay on. We galloped out of the yard and up the path. I kept my eyes forward so that I wouldn't be tempted to look behind me.

That life was now in my past. That life was gone and I was about to start a new one with a mysterious husband and no plan for the future. The people in the streets stared at us as we made our way to Eliza's. Peter stopped the horse and dropped down to the ground. He extended his arms up to me and I allowed him to help me off of the horse. He opened the gate for me and I walked up to the porch. It was weird just walking into Eliza's house and knowing that she wouldn't be there. I fiddled with the strap on my bag to help calm my nerves as Peter went to see to the horse. He also needed to go and collect his own horse from James. I sat down at the kitchen table and rubbed my temples feeling exhausted after the long day.

<<<><><>>>

(PETER)

"I promise," Lydia said and James placed their hands together. Her hands were tiny in his.

"I pronounce you husband and wife," James said then he took a step back. Peter was about to kiss her when he saw Ruben standing against one of the buildings in the town watching them with a smug look on his face. Peter wanted him to know that he wouldn't have power over Lydia now. They were married and it was up to Peter to protect her. She had done everything in her power to save him and he would repay the favor. Peter bent down to place a quick kiss on Lydia's lips. She froze at the contact making Peter pull away faster than he would have liked. He would have liked to stay there and kissed her breathless in front of the entire town. Peter saw Eliza walking over so he turned to give the two women some privacy while he talked with James. He asked James if he thought that there would be any retaliation from the town's people or Ruben or Lydia's father. He was speaking with James while listening over his shoulder and the quiet conversation going on behind him.

"He is rather handsome!" He heard the elderly lady interject and he laughed. James said that he didn't think the town's people would do anything but he also suggested that they get out as soon as possible. Peter promised to leave within a day or two. Then he turned around to Lydia and cleared his throat.

"We should be going," he said as he reached out to take her elbow. She froze at the contact and Peter felt guilty for touching her even though he knew that she would get used to it.

"Eliza has offered for us to stay in her house while she is away for a few days visiting one of her friends."

"Thank you for your kindness," Peter said as he tried to think of some way to let Eliza know that they wouldn't be staying for very long.

"I have known this dear girl for most of her life. Anything that I can do to help the two of you is my pleasure."

"We will go collect Lydia's things and then we will be over shortly. Do you need any help packing your things?"

"No, I'll be alright. I'll be leaving from here and the house will be empty by the time that you get there."

The two of them walked in silence. He didn't know what to say to her and he didn't want to startle her either. His hand brushed against hers as his arms swung at his sides. She jerked away from the contact. Peter wished that she was comfortable enough to hold his hand while they walked but he wasn't going to push her. He tucked his hand in his pocket to prevent any other accidental brushes. Her pace slowed as her house came into view and Peter spotted her father sitting on the porch in his chair.

"There she is! Everyone bow down it's the town slut!" Peter flinched at his harsh words but he didn't want to say anything in front of Lydia that might upset her.

"Lydia, why don't you go inside and gather your things while I speak to your father."

"She has nothing in there!"

"Go," Peter said gently and she inched past her father and went inside the house closing the door behind her. "I won't allow you to speak that way about my wife."

"You think she is a good and proper lady do you?!" He asked as he leaned against the railing for support so that he didn't topple over.

"She is good and that is good enough for me."

Her father let out a choking laugh and ended up in a fit of coughing.

"There is nothing good about her! She is nothing more than a whore and you were suckered into marrying her!"

Peter shook his head unwilling to continue on with the argument. The drunk wouldn't remember anyways. Peter waited silently hoping that Lydia would be out quickly.

"You know, she is a lot like her mother. Her mother didn't know what was good for her either. She was no good trash. No better than the animals."

Peter felt his temper flare as he heard Lydia's mother being talked about in such a harsh way. He knew what kind of home they had lived in. He had seen the faded bruises on Lydia's arms that she tried so hard to hide. She wouldn't ever have to hide again.

"Do you know what kind of woman you married? Do you know? Has she told you just how many men she has been with?"

"Stop it!" Peter said and he saw the smile on the wrinkled drunk face. Her father knew that he had just struck a nerve. "Do not talk about her."

"Maybe you should just leave her here. Take your chance now and walk away."

"She will be coming with me and you won't ever see her again!" Peter yelled and then he marched past her father and pushed open the front door. The kitchen was dark but he could see the closed door. "Lydia?" He called to her to see if she was in the room. There was a scraping sound and she opened the door. "Do you have your things?" Peter asked. He just wanted to get out of the house. She glanced down at the small bag that was hanging from her shoulder. He knew that he shouldn't have been surprised that she didn't have much but he couldn't help his shock. "Is that everything?" He blurted before thinking. "Then let's go," He said after she nodded. He took her hand ignoring the way that she flinched and pulled her out of the house towards the barn.

"Your father decided to give us this horse as a wedding gift. Wasn't that kind of him?" Peter asked as he opened the stalls to allow for the other animals to get out. If he had left them there they would have starved without anyone to take care of them. The chickens would just have to fend for themselves. They weren't locked in and would be able to find food. Peter tossed Lydia up onto the horse and climbed up behind her. They made their way to Eliza's house and Peter helped her off of the horse. Then he held open the gate and she walked inside the house. He watched as she closed the door and he sighed wondering if she would ever warm up to him.

Peter swung up onto the horse again and set of in the direction of the doctor's house. His own horse was being stabled there. He would see if he could put this horse there until they were ready to leave.

AUTHORS NOTE:

The best thing about being in a brace is that I can take it off to type! I hope to get more chapters up soon. Thanks for your patience and all of your kind messages!

Chapter 15

(LYDIA)

It had been hours since Peter had left with the horse. I wondered if he had taken the chance to make a break for it and get out of town. He could have left in the cover of darkness without ever looking back. Now was his chance to never have to see me again. Now was his opportunity. I sighed and pushed myself up from the table. I walked through the dimly lit kitchen to Eliza's bedroom. There was a cheerful quilt on her bed spread out across her bed I ran my finger over the delicate stitching that held the pieces of bright fabric together. I sat down and wrapped my arms around myself. I wasn't sure what to do or what to expect.

I felt a headache growing as I wondered what Peter would think of me if he ever came back. I was young when my mother died and she never told me what went on between a married couple. I stood up from the edge of the bed with a sigh and started pacing back and forth. The shadows crawled across the room as the sun went down. I was exhausted and I wondered if I should wait for Peter to get back before going to sleep. I sat down on the edge of the bed again. I felt like I could go to sleep sitting upright. After a few more minutes I decided that he probably wouldn't be coming back anyways.

I stood up to pull off my dress and my worn shoes. I folded the dress and aligned my shoes in the corner. Then wearing my underclothes I pulled back the quilt and slipped into the bed pulling the covers up to my chin. I was just about asleep when I heard the boots on the porch. I could tell that whoever was walking was trying to be quiet.

Were they expecting me to be asleep and trying to sneak up on me? I jerked upright wide awake feeling my heart start to race. My first thought was that Ruben had come for me. I wanted to dart out and hide underneath the bed. Part of me was tempted to pull the covers up over my head and hide.

No, show him that you're not afraid.

I pulled the blanket up to my chest for modesty sitting in the middle of the bed. I heard the front door ease open on well oiled hinges. The door closed quietly with an almost silent click. I couldn't hear the boots anymore and I realized that they had been removed. Straining my ears I could still hear footsteps but they were much quieter like the sound of socks. I closed my eyes to picture the kitchen and I could imagine where they were just by the sound of the footsteps. I opened my eyes and could see the slight glow from the dying embers of the fire turn bright as they were coaxed back to life. A log must have been added to the fire because the light grew even brighter.

Suddenly I saw a shadow in the doorway and the bedroom door was pushed open. My gasp of surprise was replaced by a sigh of relief when I recognized Peter's form. He looked at me and I realized that I must look a mess. Then he turned around and walked back into the kitchen. My hands were shaking as I let the blanket fall and dropped my hands at my sides. Every now and then I heard Peter move and I would strain my ears to listen for him. I listened for him to come back into the bedroom but he never did. Eventually I must have fallen asleep because when I opened my eyes it was morning.

Peter wasn't in the bedroom with me. I eased out of the bed and tiptoed across the floor trying to be as quiet as possible. I leaned around the door frame to look into the kitchen expecting to see him sitting in one of the chairs but he wasn't there. He wasn't asleep in the rocker in front of the fireplace and he wasn't sprawled out on the bench in the corner. I tiptoed through the rest of the house hoping to find him somewhere. I crawled up the ladder that led to the small loft where Eliza had dried her herbs and stored things. When I didn't see Peter their either I knew that he had taken the chance to escape.

He must have waited for me to go to sleep then he had gone into town and taken the horses and left. It shouldn't have surprised me but that didn't make it hurt any less. I descended the ladder slowly. I could hear the sound of hooves out front going down the street and for a moment I thought it might be him. I sprinted for the door and yanked it open racing outside.

In my haste I didn't see Peter sleeping on the porch and I crashed right over him. I fell to the ground with a cry of surprise and he jumped awake grabbing me and pinning me down on the wooded planks. He was on top of me with his hand at my throat and a murderous rage in his eyes. His body pressed against every inch of mine effectively trapping me. I could feel the heat rolling off of him through my thin night dress. I stared into his wild eyes terrified and he released me immediately rolling off of me and scrambled away. He sat with his back against the door frame and shoved an angry hand through his hair.

"Lydia, I'm so sorry," He whispered as I stared up at the roof too shocked to move. "Are you alright?" He asked.

"I'm fine," I whispered with a shaking voice that betrayed just how afraid I had been. He leaned forward on his toes but I still didn't move. He looked down at me and I wanted to curl into a ball.

"I slept out here to keep watch just in case anything happened. I didn't expect... I didn't know... I was startled and that's why I grabbed you."

I sat up slowly and realized that I was still in my underthings. I felt my face grow hot and I wished that I had a blanket or something to cover myself up with. I wrapped my arms around my waist wishing that I could go back in time just a few moments. I would have put on clothes. I would have stayed in the house. I would have slowly opened the front door instead of racing out like a crazy girl.

"Are you sure that you're alright?" He asked again and I felt my cheeks grow even warmer as he looked me over.

"I'm fine," I said looking anywhere but his face. I didn't want to know if he was looking at me. If Peter noticed my embarrassment he didn't comment on it.

"I am so sorry," He repeated and I couldn't take it anymore so I stood up and went inside the house. I walked straight to the back bedroom where I had kept my things and pulled on my dress. I wound my hair up tight into a bun at the back of my head and then I went outside to see if there were any eggs from the chickens. I dug around in the nest and pulled out four large eggs. I put them into my pocket and went down into the cellar to see if there was any milk or bread. To my surprise the cellar was stocked like Eliza had expected guests. I pulled out a few things then went up the stairs closing the door behind me. I cracked the eggs and dropped them into the pan. I poked at the embers in the fireplace to get them back to life and set the pan over the flame. I stirred the mixture.

"Smells good," Peter said over my shoulder and I jumped at his closeness. I hadn't heard him approach.

"It's not much but it will do," I said as I stepped to the side to allow just a few inches between us.

"What can I do to help?"

At first I didn't understand his question. It was a strange concept to me that a man would want to help in the kitchen. It was woman's work. It was a woman's responsibility to prepare the food.

"I'm almost done," I stuttered as I flipped the eggs over looking at the bright yellow mixture. They popped and sizzled as they cooked. To my relief he stepped away from me. There was a clatter of dishes as he laid them out on the table. I brought the heavy pan over and placed most of the eggs on his plate. Even though there were four spots at the table he had placed his plate next to mine instead of across the table from each other. I didn't question his decision as I scooped the rest of the eggs onto my plate. I set the pan aside to let it cool and when I returned to the table he had two thick slices of bread on my plate. Each piece had jam and my cup had milk in it. He was then slathering jam on his own pieces of bread and pouring his own cup of milk. When he saw me standing there he came over to pull my chair out for me. I sat down as he eased the chair to the table. Then he sat down right next to me.

He reached for my hand and I was reluctant to let him take it. He didn't comment as he bowed his head to pray over the food. His prayer was quick and he released my hand. I let it drop down into my lap.

"Are you sure you don't want some of this?" He asked as he gestured to his eggs piled high.

"No thank you," I said as I picked up my fork.

"You must have a lot of confidence in me if you think that I can eat all of this every day." He said as he scooped a large fork full. He glanced at the pile of eggs on my plate and shook his head but didn't say anything as he continued eating.

We finished our breakfasts in silence other than the sound of our forks bumping against the plate. Once our food was finished Peter reached over for my plate as I stood with it in my hand. I was reluctant to let it go as he eased it from my grasp and started on cleaning up the dishes. He took the dishes over to the wash water and rolled up his sleeves as he started working. I started on tidying up the kitchen and putting the remaining bread and milk away. Down in the cellar I noticed that Eliza was getting low on jam. I knew of a nearby berry patch that always had sweet berries that were excellent for jam. I could make her a batch to help repay her for her kindness of allowing us to stay in her home.

"Do you have any plans for the day?" Peter asked as I returned to the kitchen. He had the dishes drying on a towel.

"I thought I might go pick some berries," I replied looking anywhere but him. "What were you planning on doing?"

"Whatever you're doing," He said as he wiped his hands.

"I know where she might have a few baskets that we could use."

I climbed up the steps to the loft and found the baskets. I looped them over my arm as I climbed back down. He reached over and took the baskets from me and hooked them over his own arm.

"Are you ready to go?" He asked and I nodded. I noticed that he had his sword strapped to his waist. He must have gotten it while I was up in the loft collecting the baskets. Peter walked in front of me to open the front door for me. I darted out in front of him and listened as he latched the door behind us. Together we set out across the yard with me leading the way.

I walked the familiar path that lead to the thick forests that surrounded the town. As we walked I couldn't shake the feeling that we were being followed. I realized that it must just be Peter walking behind me. There was just the sound of our footsteps and then Peter started whistling. He sounded just like a bird as he let out a cheerful tune. I couldn't help but smile as we walked. I led him to the patch and took the basket as he offered it to me. The two of us set to work gathering the berries.

I let my thoughts race as I settled into the monotony of the work. My basket was about half full when I caught one of the thorns with my hand. I hissed as I yanked my arm away digging the thorn in deeper.

"Did you get a thorn?" He asked as he abandoned his basket and was at my side. I stepped back and he reached to seize my hand. I tried to pull my arm away but he held firm. To my amazement his large fingers managed to get the thorn and pull it out of my palm. Then he pressed his finger against the cut to stop the bleeding and I hissed at the sting.

"It will hurt for awhile," He said a moment later after he released my hand. I pulled it back to look at the little cut that had stopped bleeding.

"Thank you," I said glancing up to look him in the eye. I realized how close we were standing and I saw something glowing in his eyes. It was a look that Ruben had given me many times and I knew what Peter was thinking. I froze as he reached to cup my cheek with is hand. I closed my eyes and he let his hand drop and took a step away. All of a sudden I felt like he had slapped me. I opened my eyes to see him retreating to where his basket was sitting next to the bush. All of a sudden everything that had been bottled up over the past few days boiled over.

"Do I disgust you that much?!" I yelled at him as he walked away. He paused and turned to look at me with a confused expression on his face. I felt the angry hot tears roll down my cheeks but I didn't bother to wipe them away.

"What?"

"You can't even bring yourself to touch me!"

He took a step towards me and I took an involuntary step backwards. "Every time I get close to you, you step away."

"I don't mean to," I said as the tears dripped down my chin. Peter looked me in the eye and closed the distance between us in one stride. His lips claimed mine and his arms wrapped around my waist pulling me up against him. I wrapped my arms around his neck as one of his hands reached to pull the pins out of my hair. It dropped down my back and he plunged his hands into the red mass. His tongue danced against my lips as he took another step forward pressing my back against the tree.

"You don't disgust me," He whispered and moved back to my lips. Kissing me deeper and deeper. I was breathless when he pulled away. I was trembling in his arms and I was grateful that he was holding me so close. My knees felt like they would collapse if I tried to stand on my own. I was amazed at his gentleness as he held me tightly. Ruben had always been rough as he pulled me close. My thoughts of Ruben were chased away as Peter's lips found mine again.

Chapter 16

(Lydia)

"I want to show you something," I said to Peter later that day as he was helping me wash the berries that we had picked. The picked berries were brought in by the basket load and then I would put them in a bucket and wash them. After they were washed they were transferred into a large bowl and Peter would take them outside in order for them to dry. He had just brought an empty bowl back in the house after he put the berries outside to be dried in the heat.

"What is it?" He asked as he took the last bowl from me to take outside for the berries to dry. I picked up the bucket of water that was being used to rinse off the fruit. He frowned at me as I hefted the bucket. He hurried to dump the berries and return to take the bucket from me. I was reluctant to let him take it because he was still healing.

Once both of us were inside I turned my back to him and started undoing the buttons on my dress. I eased my arms out of the sleeves and let the top of the dress drop to my waist where it stayed.

"Lydia?" He said like a warning. I knew that he was confused by my actions but I had to show him the scars from the past so that I could move on to the future. He had to know what had happened to me. If he didn't understand my scars then he wouldn't ever be able to understand me. "What are you doing?"

"I need to show you something," I loosened the tie at the top of my under dress and pushed the narrow sleeves off of my shoulders as I held the dress up to my front. I heard a sharp intake of breath and I knew that Peter had seen the scars on my back. He walked across the kitchen towards me while I kept my eyes on the flowers that were in a vase on the table. I felt his gentle fingers trace one of the longer scars that ran over my shoulder blade and I flinched. "That was when I fell against the stove," I said as his fingers ran over the length of it. "At least that's what I told James when he patched me up. It did come from the stove and I did fall. My father slapped me so hard that I lost my balance and crashed into the corner. I remember laying there on the kitchen floor trying to catch my breath as my father stepped over me to walk to his room and go to sleep with a bottle."

Peter brushed my loose braid off of my shoulder and touched the scar that started at the base of my ear and traveled up past my hairline. "That one was from trying to keep my door shut. My father threw himself against it and I was thrown backwards against my bed post. I don't remember much about the rest of that night."

I felt Peter's gentle fingers on the other scars on my back and I told him the stories that went with each of them. He didn't say anything. He just listened as I explained what had happened. The entire time I kept my eyes on the flowers on the table. I didn't want to see his expression. I didn't want to know what he thought of me.

I felt his fingers under my chin as he came to stand in front of me. He lifted my face up so that I had to look at him. He leaned down to press a kiss against my lips that was as gentle as his fingers had been against my skin.

"I won't ever hurt you," He said once he pulled away. I slipped my arms through the narrow sleeves of my under dress and shrugged it up. Peter's eye caught on the yellowed bruise that was around my upper arm. "What's this one from?" He asked as he lifted my arm to look at it from a different angle. The prints of fingers were still visible in the ugly yellowed mark. He must have realized that the marks were from fingers because he wrapped his own hand around the mark. His hands were much to large and his fingers were too long to be a match.

"My father doesn't like it when I walk away from him," I said and then started to slide my arms through the sleeves on my dress. Peter let my arm go as I pulled the dress up and started doing up the buttons.

"What did Ruben do about all of this?"

"He didn't want to embarrass me so we didn't talk about it."

Peter gave a short humorless laugh that made me jump.

"That man was a coward and he didn't deserve you," He said as he dropped down into one of the chairs that were surrounding the table. "I don't deserve you," He whispered as he took my hand in his.

"You saved me just as much as I saved you. There will be no more talk about what we don't deserve."

I walked out the door to go get the berries that would be dry after their time in the heat. We had managed to pick enough for a large batch of jam that would replace Eliza's stores. There would also be enough left over to bake into a pie or some other delicious treat. I brought them inside the house and Peter helped me with the bucket. I walked him through the steps to make the jam for Eliza. I saved a bowl full of the berries and left them to the side.

While Peter was out seeing to the animals and taking care of the horses I set to work on baking the pie. It was getting dark outside when I pulled the pie out of the oven. I gasped as I saw movement out one of the side windows and burnt my fingers as I set the pie down on the table. I put my fingers in a bucket that had water in it and that helped to take the sting out. I kept my eyes locked on the window and squinted out into the evening darkness. I could have sworn that I saw someone at the window watching me. There was the sound of boots on the porch and I spun to stare at the door as Peter walked in. I released a sigh of relief and looked back to the window. Nothing had moved and there wasn't anybody out there.

"What happened?" Peter asked hearing my sigh of relief.

"I was being foolish," I said holding up my dripping fingers. The skin had already turned red and I could still feel the sting. I dropped my hand back into the water.

"Here, I have something that might help."

I stepped forward and sat down in the chair that Peter was indicating to. He then reached for my hand and I gave it to him anxious to see what he had that would take the sting out. He leaned down and pressed a kiss to each one of my fingers. I smiled at his gesture and when he looked up at me he had a new light glowing in his eyes. My hand dropped down into my lap as he placed his hands at the sides of the seat of the chair to lean forward and press his lips against mine. I smiled against his lips as he leaned closer. His kisses continued and somehow he ended up in the chair and I was sitting comfortably on his lap. One of his hands pressed against the small of my back while the other was tangled up in my hair. I was breathless when I pulled away from him. He pressed his lips against my neck and I cleared my throat trying to form coherent thoughts.

"I think the pie might be ready," I said when I remembered it cooling on the counter.

He mumbled against my skin and I slid off of his lap onto my feet. He grumbled his disapproval and I reached for the pie.

He was right. I had completely forgotten about my singed fingers.

I tucked a piece of loose hair behind my ear and started to cut through the pie. I cut each of us a slice and put them on plates. Peter was still sitting in his chair at the table watching me as I set the plate down in front of him. He picked up the fork and took a bite. The entire time his eyes followed me as I set my plate down next to his.

"How is it?"

"Delicious," He replied as he set his fork down. "But I think I might have found something that I want even more than the pie." He stood up and wrapped an arm around my waist pulling me against him. His kiss tasted like blackberry pie.

<<<><><>>>

(LYDIA)

I jerked upright and felt an arm slide down my waist as I pushed away from the warm body next to me. I toppled out of the bed and fell onto the floor pulling the blankets with me.

"Lydia?" I heard Peter's voice as I sat on the floor looking up at the bed. He was out of the bed and crouching down in front of me in an instant. "What is it?" He asked as he reached to tuck my loose hair behind my ear.

I tried to catch my breath as I looked up at the bedroom window. There was a full moon outside that was casting shadows around the yard. I could see a figure walking away from the window. I knew in an instant who the person was. I didn't need to see their face or see their clothing to know who they were. I could tell from the sickening shiver that traveled down my spine.

"Ruben," I whispered and Peter followed my gaze. He jumped to his feet and pulled on a pair of his discarded pants as he ran out of the room barefoot. I heard the front door slam behind him as he followed Ruben out into the night. I tried to calm my breathing as I waited for him to come back.

"He will come back," I whispered to myself as I tried to ignore the images that came into my mind of Ruben out there waiting for Peter in the darkness. Would sneak up behind him and run him through with his sword? Or would he could shoot him with an arrow from a distance? This was personal, it would definitely be with the sword. Ruben would want to be there when Peter died. He would want to be close to ensure that he was dead. I backed myself into the corner of the room and wrapped the blanket around myself as I tried to push images of Peter's dead body out of my mind. The images kept coming and I could see him bleeding out in the street. He would gasp for air and choke on the blood. I could imagine Ruben's smirk while he watched Peter die. Then he would come for me.

"No," I said as I tried to convince myself that everything would be alright. There was a figure in the doorway of the room and I flinched. Then I recognized Peter. I stood up and ran into his arms. "I was so worried," I said against his chest as I held onto him.

"It's alright, now."

"He was watching us," I said stating the obvious.

Peter's hand stroked over my hair calming me as I clung to him.

"We should leave," Peter said as he held me tight. He pressed a kiss against the crown of my head.

"Where will we go?" I asked tipping my head to look up at him.

"We will go to my home."

"Where is that?" I asked as I realized just how little I knew about my husband.

"Chedix," He replied. "Come back to bed," He said tugging me along with him and holding me tight in his arms.

Chapter 17

He watched as Lydia tried to hide a large yawn behind her hand. It had been a long night and even though she had pretended to be asleep Peter could tell that she had been awake for most of the night unable to relax. She thought that Ruben would be there at any moment. She saw danger lurking behind every turn and tree trunk. Peter couldn't blame her. After everything that she had told him it was a wonder that she could even make it through each day without falling apart. She had suffered a lot in her short life.

"We should be there soon," Peter said as he rode up next to her on his horse. He hoped that the news would lift her spirits.

"That's good," She replied as she shifted in the saddle. They had their own horses and their few belongings were stowed in the saddle bags. She didn't have much. Lydia flinched at the sound of a stick crunching beneath the large hooves of the horse she was riding. Her cheeks flushed red when she noticed that Peter was watching her.

He wanted to tell her that it was alright and that she didn't need to be afraid but he knew that it wouldn't make any difference. She had learned to be afraid. That was how she had stayed alive.

"Perhaps Susan will prepare a large feast for us in our honor when we arrive," He said trying to distract her again.

"Who is Susan?"

It was then that he realized that he hadn't told her much about where they were going. Peter started talking about his friends in Chedix. He wanted her to know about the family that they were going back to. His family. He told Lydia about Ellie and Ben and how they had met and what had happened to them when Ellie had been taken by Roderick. Peter spoke about the wars and the twins. He spoke of childhood memories back when he was growing up with Ben.

Peter knew that she was listening so he kept talking. Any story that came to his mind was shared just so they didn't have to travel in silence. He told her about the children and how amazing he thought they were. When she laughed after one of his stories he knew that she was paying attention.

"It sounds like paradise. Why would you ever leave that place?" She asked interrupting him and he immediately thought about blonde hair and dark blue eyes. He didn't know how she would react to his story about Ryah and he didn't want to tell her. He didn't want her to question him or think that he didn't want to be with her. Ryah had moved on and she was with Torin. Peter knew that. As he looked over at Lydia he realized that he had moved on too.

"I left because I needed a change," He said with a smile. It was mostly true. Lydia returned his smile which told him that she had believed him.

Peter knew that going to Chedix was the right thing. Nobody would know Lydia's past there. It would be a fresh start for them. She wouldn't have people watching her in the street and seeing her as the daughter of a drunk. People wouldn't see her as the little girl in dirty clothes covered with bruises. People wouldn't look down at their feet as she walked by because they were too ashamed to look her in the eyes.

Chedix would be the perfect place for them to begin their lives together.

<<<><><>>>

(Lydia)

I felt my mouth drop open as I looked at the village in front of us. I wasn't seeing the paradise that Peter had described. The village locked as though it had barely survived an attack. There were freshly turned graves with dark soil heaped up in mounds. I looked at Peter and his expression was a mirror of my own.

"What happened?" I asked him even though I knew that he wouldn't know the answer.

He didn't reply as he spurred his horse forward. I followed closely behind him. All around us were signs of a battle. The charred remains of houses were along the side of the street. Their dark frames stood like skeletons. The houses that were still standing had doors kicked in and shattered windows. Fences were torn over and gardens had been destroyed.

"Peter!" Someone called and Peter dropped down off his horse as there was a flash of red hair and a woman dove into his arms.

"What happened Ellie?" He asked as he held onto her tightly.

"We were attacked," She stated the obvious as she pulled away and her brown eyes met mine. There was a look of surprise but then she turned her attention back to Peter. I realized that this was the woman that he had told me about in his stories. She was the strong one who had saved her husband from an evil man.

"Where is everyone? Are they alright? Where are the children?" He asked each question tumbling out of his mouth before Ellie had the chance to answer any of them. "Where is Ben?"

"The children are alright and the town is doing well. We are trying to get everything put back together. Ben was injured but he is doing a lot better now."

"How did this happen?" He asked

"It was those men who took Ryah and Anna."

"Kyle's group?"

She nodded.

"I had an encounter with them as well," He said and he looked over at me. Ellie followed his gaze and she smiled.

"Hello," She said walking towards me. I dropped down out of the saddle and stood in front of her. She was quite a bit shorter than me.

"Hello," I said but I didn't know what to do. Ellie surprised me when she reached forward and wrapped her arms around me holding me against her in a tight hug. I slowly wrapped my arms around her shoulders because I didn't know what else to do. Peter smiled at me over Ellie's shoulder.

"I am Ellie."

"My name is Lydia," I replied when she released me and tried to give her what I thought was my best smile. I had to remind myself that this woman didn't know me. She didn't see me for my past. All she knew was that Peter had brought me in. If Peter was her friend she had to be decent.

"Peter!!" A shrill voice called and out of nowhere there was a little girl. Peter caught her as she jumped towards him and threw her up in the air.

"I've caught myself a little fairy!" Peter exclaimed as he set the girl down on his shoulder. She wrapped an arm around his face and grabbed onto his chin. Her large blue eyes smiled down at me from Peter's shoulder.

"I'm not a fairy," She explained to me.

"You must be Thea," I said looking up at her. Her eyes widened in shock. "Peter told me all about you."

She blushed and pulled Peter's hair.

"What did you say?!" She demanded playfully as he howled in mock agony.

"I told her what a nice little girl you were, but now she isn't going to believe me," Peter said as he lifted her down to the ground. Thea looked up at me with a shy smile and stepped forward towards me. She extended her finger towards me and a crouched down in front of her. She cupped her hands around her mouth and leaned in to whisper in my ear.

"You're really pretty," She whispered and I was shocked as I leaned away. Then she was gone. She ran down the street and disappeared into a house that was still standing.

"Where's Petey?" Peter asked looking around. I remembered that the little boy was Thea's twin and his namesake.

"I'm sure that he will turn up at some point," Ellie explained. "Let's get your things taken care of then we can go see Ben."

A short time later after we had our belongings in Peter's house we were standing at the foot of a large bed. There was a man in the bed and he was huge. He was tall and strong and had dark curly hair. I could see the resemblance between him and Thea. Ellie took his hand and he opened his blue eyes. I realized that this must be Peter's best friend and Ellie's husband, Ben. Once his gaze settled on Peter a large grin lit up his face.

"I was wondering when you would come back?" He said and tried to sit up. Ellie placed a small hand on his chest and he stopped trying to get up.

"What happened here?" Peter asked.

"It was night when they attacked. They started burning houses before we realized what was happening. It was a short battle and the men were defeated."

"I should have been here," Peter said.

Ben and Ellie looked at me then back at Peter. "You couldn't have been here, not after what happened."

I thought that Ellie might have been talking about me but I realized that there must be more to the story about why Peter left than he had told me. I wanted to ask him about what they were talking about but I decided that I would ask him later.

"Who are you?" I was pulled back into the conversation when I realized that Ben was talking to me. I reached over and took Peter's hand.

"I'm...."

"She's my wife," Peter said for me. I looked at him gratefully. I knew that we were with his friends but I still felt self conscious and uncomfortable.

"Your wife?" Ellie asked.

"I saved her from Kyle and his men, well, actually she saved me."

I blushed as I remembered how he had fought off Orvil even after I had stabbed him.

Ben tipped back his head and laughed which made me jump. "That does sound like our Peter," He said teasing. "Needing a girl to come to his rescue."

"And what's the matter with that?" Ellie asked with her hands on her hips. Ben took her hand and tugged her down so that she was sitting on the bed next to him.

"Absolutely nothing," Ben replied.

"We saved each other," I interjected and Peter gave my hand a squeeze.

"That's how it should be," said Ellie. "You should get some rest," she said to Ben as she leaned down to press a kiss on his lips.

"All I do is rest," He complained like a child.

"You were shot with an arrow."

"I'm nearly recovered," he whined.

"Don't make me injure you further," Ellie growled and Ben smiled at her. "Now, if you go to sleep I might come visit you later," She said mischievously.

Immediately his eyes closed and Ellie leaned down to kiss his lips again. Then she stood up and the three of us left the room. Ellie and Peter chatted and I listened to their conversation as I followed behind them. We walked into a large kitchen where there was a massive stone fireplace. The smell of fresh baked bread filled the room and I took a large breath of the sweet air.

"I see that Susan is still baking," Peter said as he walked towards the large loaves of bread that were cooling on the table.

"We have actually been preparing for her wedding."

"Wedding?" Peter said with a knife in his hand about to slice through the loaf.

"She's going to marry Jack, that man from Rollo's group."

"When?"

"They were going to get married a few days ago but with the attack and everything that has happened they have pushed it back."

Peter placed a large piece of steaming bread in front of me then he cut a slice for Ellie and then one for himself. I thanked him and took a seat at the table. The bread did smell amazing and I realized just how hungry I was after all of our traveling.

"Now," Ellie said gesturing at the two of us as Peter sat next to me. "There is a story here and I want to hear it."

Chapter 18

(LYDIA)

I glanced over my shoulder to look at the small house behind me. Peter had been thrilled to learn that his house had survived the attack. The windows were smashed and the place was a disaster but it was still standing. We had unpacked our few things and then cleaned for most of the night. When the last piece of broken glass was cleared out of the way we decided that it was time to go to bed and leave the rest for the morning. Peter held me in his arms all night long and I realized that I was finally home.

The next morning I awoke alone and based on the brightness outside I realized that it was late morning already. I had overslept after being awake for most of the night cleaning. Peter was already gone and I knew that he had wanted to let me get some rest. I climbed out of bed humming to myself as I straightened the covers. I left the bedroom and pulled back the blankets that we had hung in front of the shattered windows. The little house looked different in the sunlight. I glanced around the room and my eyes fell on a small vase that was stuffed with bright wildflowers. I smiled at the thought of Peter picking those for me.

I tidied up a few of the things that we had left the night before and pulled on my dress. Ellie had sent us with some of Susan's thick bread and a little jar of jam. I smeared the jam on a slice of the bread that was still soft and bit into it. My eyes closed and I decided that I would have to ask Susan for the secret of making such delicious bread. I figured that she might be baking the bread for that evening's meal right now. She would probably let me watch. I tied my hair into a braid and set out in the direction of her house.

I jumped in surprise as the door that I was reaching for burst open. Petey burst through the doorway and stomped past me letting the door slam shut behind him. His little shoulders were slumped and he kicked at a pebble on the ground with his toe as he walked. One big kick sent the pebble flying and it smacked the side of the house that was in front of him with a loud thunk.

"What's the matter?" I asked him and he shook his head looking at the ground to avoid looking at me. I walked over to where he stood expecting him to run away from me but he was holding completely still other than the shaking of his shoulders. I knew how it felt to have an adult towering over me so I crouched down in front of him and waited for his eyes to meet mine. I reached out to take his hand. "I wish that you would talk to me," I said softly.

Eventually his eyes rose up to mine and I held his gaze for a few seconds then he sniffed and looked away from me pulling his hand back. Still he didn't turn and run like I had expected. His eyes darted around for a second and he took a deep breath.

"Do you feel like I stole Peter away from you?" I asked. I didn't know what was wrong or what had made the little boy so angry.

"No," He mumbled quietly and wiped his nose on his sleeve.

"Do you not like me?"

He shook his head quickly and the hair on his forehead flopped back and forth.

"Then what is the matter?"

"I want someone to play with," He said simply and I was surprised. His little outburst was caused by loneliness. I understood loneliness.

"Would it be alright if I played with you?" I asked and his eyebrows rose up and he finally looked me in the eye holding my gaze.

"You want to play with me?" He asked.

"Of course!" I said excitedly not knowing what we would do. I hadn't ever spent time with a small child. I looked around and my eyes fell on the barn. I remembered being his age, I had been fascinated with horses. "Why don't we go on a ride?" I asked him and his eyes got wide.

We made our way towards the barn and I felt his hand slip into mine as we walked. We went into the barn together and he waited while I got the horse saddled up and climbed up on its back. Petey extended his arm and I helped him get up in the saddle in front of me.

"Where are we going to go?" He asked as he straightened out his back to see over the horse's neck.

"Where do you want to go?"

"To the river!" he said and pointed in the direction of the trees that were on the other side of a large grassy field.

<<<><><>>>

(PETER)

"Do you think there could be another attack?"

"I have no idea what to expect," Ben said as he stood up from his chair. Peter knew that Ellie would be furious that he was out of bed but Peter wasn't about to tell Ben to go back. Ben had managed to pull his boots on and they were making their way outside. The two friends had been talking about how Kyle's men could rally and come back for a second attack. Peter didn't think that it was likely because they had been victorious in the first battle.

Kyle had been sent by Errit to seek revenge on Rollo for betraying the marriage contract with Errit's sister Grey. Ellie saved Rollo's wife from Kyle's men and that was what brought Chedix into the battle. Ben knew that Errit's temper wouldn't be defeated by losing one battle. He thought that Errit would come back for a second attack. Because of this fear, Ben was encouraging everyone to stay close to town. Scouts were sent out and placed around the perimeter to let the town know if there was anything suspicious going on.

Peter couldn't help but notice the differences in the town. The houses that had once held so much promise of a new life had been easily destroyed. Peter knew that they could be rebuilt but it was still shocking to see how easily something someone had worked so hard on could be destroyed. Many of the houses and the possessions that were inside them were every-thing that the town's people owned. Ben and Ellie were doing their best to make things work. The people of Elondra had sent many things to help the people of Chedix. Ellie's parents had made the journey and they were visiting with their daughter and the children.

"Ben!" Ellie's voice rang out behind them and Peter braced himself to be reprimanded. "Have you seen Petey?" She asked.

Both men shook their heads and she spun around to look out around the town to see if she could spot him. He wasn't out in the fields and he wasn't in the street. Peter knew that the little boy could have been anywhere. He was adventurous and not afraid of anything.

"Do you need help looking for him?" Peter asked and Ellie nodded.

"It would be best if everyone would stick close to town," Ben said and Ellie seemed to notice that he was out of bed when he should have been resting. Before she could open her mouth to scold him for being out and about, Ben turned to Peter. "Would you go out to look for him while the two of us look around the houses? He could be playing in any of the abandoned houses."

Peter nodded and Ben put his arm around his wife so that she could support him while they walked around the few houses that were still standing. Peter could hear them asking the neighbors if they had seen anything as he went to get a horse. Once in the stable, he noticed that Lydia's horse was gone. He checked the yard and looked around the field. Peter saddled up and climbed on his horse. He went back to Ellie and Ben.

"Have you seen Lydia?" He asked. Neither of them had seen her.

"Maybe she has Petey?" Ellie said hopefully and tightened her grip on Ben's hand.

"I'll ride out and see if I can find them," Peter said and pointed his horse away from town.

<<<><><>>>

(LYDIA)

I loved the feeling of the wind through my hair as we flew along the path that twisted around the trees. The sunlight burst through the leaves and flashed across my face. Petey was sitting in front of me leaning low in the saddle. His feet were tucked under my legs to keep his legs from flopping around. We passed the river and went deeper into the thick forest that surrounded Chedix. The path became rough and so we slowed down to a slow walk. Several times low hanging trees forced us to duck and I was grateful that we had slowed down.

"We should probably get back home," I said to Petey as I noticed the lengthening shadows on the ground. The sun was beginning to set and I wasn't familiar enough with the area to find my way in the dark.

"Alright," Petey said. He didn't bother to cover up the disappointment in his voice.

"We can go riding on a different day if you would like," I said hoping that it would help cheer him up.

We trotted forward and I could hear the sound of another horse behind us. I didn't want Petey to know that I was getting nervous so I spurred the horse forward and leaned lower in the saddle. Petey cheered as the wind blew through his hair and he tucked his hands into the horse's mane to hold on.

My heart was in my throat when we finally burst out of the trees and flew towards the town. I slowed down as we approached and looked around behind me. When nothing came out of the trees behind us I realized that I was scaring myself over nothing. I laughed at myself and tucked my hair behind my ears.

I noticed that Petey was happily chatting at me and I tried to pay attention. I took him up to the house and helped him off of the saddle. He gave me a huge smile and wrapped his arms around my neck thanking me for the ride. Then he released me and slid off of the saddle onto the ground. He ran into the house and I turned towards the barn. Once inside I dropped out of the saddle and started the process of getting the saddle off of the horse and giving her a brush down after the ride. She tucked her nose into a feed bag and stood still while I set to work.

The barn door opened causing both of us to jump as Peter walked in. I leaned my face against the horse's shoulder as I took a deep breath calming myself.

"You scared me," I said laughing at myself.

"Where were you?" He demanded as he walked towards me. I glanced at him and noticed his disheveled hair that looked like he had shoved a hand through it more than once.

"I went out for a ride with Petey, I saw him and he looked really sad and he told me that he wanted someone to play with. I offered to take him out for a ride to cheer him up."

"Without telling anyone?"

"I didn't realize that I needed to ask permission. I should have asked his parents first, I'm sorry." I realized that Petey's parents had probably been looking for him. We had been gone for the majority of the afternoon and the sun had practically set. I started brushing the horse again and his arms shot out grabbing me and spinning me around by my shoulders. I gasped in surprise as I stared up at him. I was frozen in place as he took a deep breath.

I could tell that he was trying to remain calm but that he was struggling to do so. /he kept my at arms length and didn't try to get any closer. He opened his mouth and for an instant I saw the face of my father. I felt my father's hands gripping my shoulders tightly. I felt the specks of my father's spit flying from his mouth as he leaned in close to my face and screamed at me. My heart sped up and I could hear my blood pounding in my ears. Tears welled up in my eyes as I realized my mistake. I couldn't trust anyone.

I thought that Peter was different but it was becoming clear to me that all men were the same.

All men would hurt me.

I shrugged out of his grasp and took a few steps away from him.

"Lydia!" He said to me as I walked out of the barn. I felt his hand on my wrist to make me stop.

"Let go of me!" I screamed at him and his grip immediately loosened releasing me. I raced out of the barn sprinting towards home. Peter's home.

I would grab my things and leave. We had just barely unpacked yesterday but I knew where all of my things were. I could easily shove them into a sack and be gone before anyone realized what happened. I charged through the house and yanked open the door of the bedroom without bothering to light a fire. I felt the drawer handle and pulled it open grabbing my dress and holding it over my arm as I got my other articles of clothing and shoved them into a sack. As I spun around to go out of the house I saw a dark figure leaning against the door frame. The last rays of the setting sun behind them only let me see their silhouette but that was enough.

"Hello Lydia," Ruben drawled.

AUTHOR'S NOTE:

I feel like one of those flaky writers who just fizzles out towards the end of a story and you wonder if they're dead or alive because they used to be better at updating. My schedule is busy and doesn't leave much time to write anything other than the articles and essays that are due during the week. But, I will not leave you hanging. The story will be finished in a chapter or two. I also have the next story started but I want to get a few chapters ahead so that you don't have to wait so long between updates. Thank you for your patience and all of your support!

Chapter 19

(LYDIA)

"What are you doing here?" I asked trying to hide how afraid I was.

He laughed and let the door close behind him as he entered my home. The room was cast into darkness and it took a second for my eyes to adjust to see him moving towards me. I told my feet to go backwards but they didn't listen. I was rooted to the spot.

I saw a dark shape moving towards me. His arm, as he reached out. I felt his fingers brush along my jaw and I could smell his foul breath. He had been drinking. It was a surprise, he was always drinking. My leaving probably hadn't helped.

I wished for Peter to come into the house at that moment. I prayed to anyone who would listen and hoped that someone would walk through the door. Why had I screamed at Peter to get away from me? Why had I behaved in the way that I did? Telling him that he was just like my father wasn't only rude, it was untrue. Ruben leaned towards me and I found my courage as I took a few steps backwards out of his reach and slammed the bedroom door in his face. I leaned against it trying to brace with my legs.

It wasn't any use. Ruben was much larger than I was and he was so much stronger. His anger fueled by the drink. I knew that he would be able to knock the door down with little effort. He slammed his hand flat against the wood with a loud crack that made me tremble. "You think that you can hide from me?!" He demanded his words slurring as he yelled. "I am your Master! I will always find you no matter where you go."

The door knob jiggled and I wanted to close my eyes and pretend that this wasn't happening. But it was happening and denying it wouldn't do me any good. I took a deep breath to calm my pounding heart. Ruben could bust down the door and he would beat me then he would move on to the rest of the people in Chedix. There was no telling how much damage he would do before he was stopped. I imagined little Petey's face bruised and I knew what I had to do.

"You're right!" I called to him through the door hoping that in his drunken state he wouldn't notice how my voice was shaking. "You are my Master. I don't know how I was so blind."

I eased away from the door and watched as the door handle spun. Ruben pushed the door open slowly and I stood up straighter trying to look confident and sure of myself. I knew that he couldn't see me very well in the dark but standing taller made me feel better. It made me feel strong instead of weak.

"You're right, Ruben."

He reached for me and I felt his hand on my waist. He stepped closer and I wanted to run but I stood still. He pressed a kiss against my neck and I didn't squirm away from him.

"Why did you leave me?" He asked sounding like he was going to cry.

"He fooled me. Peter fooled me."

Ruben wrapped his arms around me holding me close. I felt the bile rising up in my stomach.

"I thought that he could protect me but I was wrong," I continued as tears clouded in my eyes. It was a good thing it was dark, Ruben didn't tolerate crying. "Only you can protect me. You're my Master."

I put my hands his face pulling him to my lips to kiss him. When he tried to deepen the kiss I let him. For the first time, I didn't stop him. I let him kiss me and felt his hands travel over my body. Suddenly his roaming hands stopped and he pulled away from me.

"You're lying!" He roared and his hand flew towards me connecting with the side of my head. I fell backwards smashing into the shelf causing everything to go black.

<<<><><>>>

(PETER)

"What happened?" Ben said and Peter looked up to see Ben standing in front of him with his arms crossed over his chest.

"I found Petey and Lydia. They were together and they are safe."

"And?"

"Lydia said that I was just like her father and she stormed off."

"What did you say to her?"

"Just that she needed to stay close. What are you now? My father?" Peter asked as he walked around Ben. He didn't have to give Ben an explanation. "We will figure this out. She just needs some time to cool off."

"You should go talk to her," Ben said as he fell into step beside Peter.

"She wants to be alone, and I don't know what to say to her."

Peter fiddled with the sword strapped to his waist as he walked with Ben. Peter knew that he was thinking about the time that Ellie had run away from him. She was captured and their lives were in chaos for months. Peter wondered what he would do in that situation. If Lydia was taken away from him he knew that he would be miserable. Peter sighed and stopped walking. Ben paused to and looked over at him with a smirk on his face.

"You think that I should just go and apologize to her don't you?"

"I think that you should go and talk to her," Ben replied. Peter sighed again and shoved a hand through his hair.

"Fine," He said and spun around.

"Hello Peter."

There was no mistaking that voice. Peter tightened his grip on his sword as he faced Ruben who was standing about ten feet away. He couldn't believe that he didn't hear him approach. Ben's hand immediately went to the sword that was at his waist but Peter knew that it was too soon for Ben to get in a fight. One wrong move and he would be killed because of his previous injury.

"He's mine," Peter said and lunged at Ruben with his sword held high. Ruben matched him swing for swing. Each jab was countered by an equally forceful block. By the way that Ruben staggered Peter realized that he was drunk. A drunk man was a dangerous opponent. They didn't think of injuring them self in the fight. All they they cared about was their rage. It made them strong and difficult to beat.

Ruben's sword flew through the air and Peter managed to block it just in time to prevent it from hitting him. Ruben's movements were awkward and difficult to predict.

"Is that the best that you can do?" Peter asked hoping to get a reaction from Ruben. He wasn't disappointed as the drunken man roared and charged forward as Peter danced out of the way distracting him and getting him to use his energy. If Peter could just outlast Ruben he would win the fight. Ruben had been drinking and that made his swings inaccurate but they were still powerful.

A well placed swing caught Peter's shoulder tearing his shirt and nicking his arm. He felt the blood drip down his arm as he blocked another blow. If he could just keep blocking then Ruben would tire and slow down.

A few more swings and Ruben took a step back panting and he tightened his grip on his sword before coming in for another swing. Peter stepped towards Ruben getting closer to him causing him to step backwards and stumble. Peter took advantage of the distraction and caught Ruben's cheek with the tip of his sword. It wasn't supposed to be a fatal wound but it would make Ruben angry. Ruben yelled swinging his sword too far forward and Peter managed to block at just the right time to knock the sword out of Ruben's hand. Ben picked up the sword and held it at his side.

Ruben lunged for the sword and Peter kicked his legs out from underneath him. Ruben fell down on the ground on his back. Peter was surprised to hear him burst out laughing. Ruben struggled to breath as he choked on his laughter. Ruben held his hands up at his sides in surrender trying to look serious. When Peter looked at him he lost it and bust out laughing again. Peter didn't understand what he found so funny. He had been defeated. He was on the ground without a weapon or a way to protect himself. Peter lifted his sword and pointed it directly at Ruben's throat. Just a few more inches and that would be the end. Peter wondered if he could do it.

"I won!" Ruben yelled and tipped his head back laughing.

<<<><><>>>

(LYDIA)

I groaned at the pain in my head as I sat up slowly. I looked around but it was dark and I was confused. The thick smokey smell filled my nose and I coughed trying to get a breath of fresh air. Slowly I got to my feet leaning on the wall for support so I wouldn't fall over.

Where was Ruben?

I squinted through the darkness trying to make out any shapes but I couldn't see anything. I noticed a faint glow under the bedroom door and I reached for the door handle but it was burning hot. I jerked my arm back and cradled it against my chest. I pulled part of my skirt up and used it to block my hand as I turned the door handle. The kitchen was full of light from the flames that were dancing at the windows. I took a step back to avoid the flames that were just outside the door. It looked like Ruben had placed a burning blanket right outside the door.

"No!" I cried as I jumped over the flames and raced for the front door. I slammed against it shoving it with my shoulder trying to get it open but it was no use. Ruben had locked me in from the outside. I pounded my fists against the door hoping that someone would hear me.

"Ruben!" I screamed hoping that he would be on the outside of the door listening. "Ruben let me out!" It was useless. Even if he was outside he would let me die. He wanted me to die. The flames crawled down the wall beneath the window and I ran back to the bedroom closing the door behind me and stuffing my sack with the clothes down on the floor at the base of the door to help keep some of the smoke out. My eyes were watering as I pulled back the blanket that was at the small window in the bedroom to try to let some of the smoke out. I tried to get my head out to get a fresh breath of the night air.

I cursed the small window that wasn't wide enough to fit my shoulders through. If I could just squeeze through it I would be free. I tried again to climb out it but no matter how I twisted and turned I couldn't fit.

Where was Peter?

Why hadn't he come for me?

I dropped down to the floor to get below the smoke and try to breath. When Peter saw the flames he would come and save me. I knew that he would come and save me. I just had to stay awake long enough for him to find me.

<<<><><>>>

(PETER)

"Peter!" Ben yelled and took off running with a hand pressed to his side. Peter didn't want to look away from the figure at his feet. "Peter now!" Ben screamed and Peter looked away from Ruben to see a glow in the sky. It was a fire and Peter instantly knew what was burning. He left Ruben on the ground with his hands up like a coward. The orange red haze climbed into the sky and Peter sprinted faster towards his home.

He came to a stop next to Ben and raised his arm in front of his face to block the heat. "What happened?" He said as he caught his breath.

"Where's Lydia?!" Ben demanded and Peter's blood ran cold. Without thinking he sprinted towards the house and kicked down the door that had been bolted from the outside.

Ruben.

Ruben had locked her inside and set the place ablaze to kill her.

"Lydia!" Peter screamed as the flames lunged at him in the open doorway. He charged forward towards the bedroom shoving the door open and his foot collided with something. He dropped down and felt in front of him. It was her. He grabbed hold of her pulling her into his arms holding her close. What was left of the house groaned and Peter wondered when it would come down. He sprinted towards the door through the flames that licked at his body.

"Peter stop!" Ellie yelled and she attacked him with a blanket. Peter realized that his clothes had small flames on them. The blanket snuffed out the flames and he looked down at Lydia with streaming eyes.

"She's not breathing," He gasped and started coughing. He had to put Lydia down on the ground because he couldn't breath. Ellie pushed Peter out of the way as he dropped down to his hands and knees and started retching from the smoke. Peter watched with streaming eyes as Ben and Ellie crowded around Lydia.

"Help her!" He wheezed through his burning throat. "Please help her!"

Chapter 20

(PETER)

He watched the steady rise and fall of Lydia's chest and he was grateful for each breath that she took. Ellie and Ben had worked a miracle and had helped her to breathe again. Peter held onto her hand as he sat on the edge of the large bed. Ellie and Ben had graciously allowed Lydia to take over their bed because Peter's house had burned down to the ground. Lydia was the one thing that had been salvaged from the flames.

Everything else was dust.

Peter wasn't concerned with what had burned. Those things felt like they were from his past life. A time when he was lonely. As he looked at Lydia's eyes flutter in her sleep he realized that all the things he cared about were in his future.

He stood up and paced around the room. So much had happened in the past day that it felt like it had been a lifetime. After the fight, Ruben had disappeared. Peter hoped that he wouldn't come back but he knew that Ruben could turn up when least expected. When Peter changed Lydia into a clean nightgown he saw the dark bruise on her shoulder from throwing herself against the front door to get it opened. Ruben had locked it from the outside ensuring that she wouldn't be able to escape. The windows had been too small to fit through. Peter made a note to himself to make the windows in his new home larger and to put in a door at the back just in case. He shoved a hand through his hair as he listened to Lydia breathing. So many things went wrong and could have gone much worse.

Lydia mumbled something and Peter was back at her side with her hand in his just in case she opened her eyes. He wanted to see her eyes open and looking at him. He wanted to tell her how much he loved her and how much she meant to him. He wanted to tell her that he loved her with everything that he had. He wanted to say that everything would be alright and they would be together. But he didn't know for sure. He didn't know if they would be alright. He didn't know if Lydia would ever open her eyes again or if she would be alright.

<<<><><<>>>

(LYDIA)

I could hear the steady sound of boots marching across the room. Every now and then there was a small scraping sound and I knew that whomever was pacing had spun around to make the trek back across the room. I forced my eyes open and had to blink a few times to clear them. I immediately saw Peter with his back towards me and his hand up to his face as he paced. He was absentmindedly rubbing his chin that had at least two days worth of stubble on it.

That didn't concern me. What did catch my eye was the large bandage that was wrapped around his arm.

"What happened to your arm?" I croaked and tried to clear my raw throat.

Peter was at my side in an instant taking both of my hands in his. "Lydia" He breathed as he looked at me. I tried to take a deep breath but my chest hurt terribly. I must have groaned from the pain. "Your ribs will be sore for a while," He said as he sat down in the chair next to me without releasing my hands.

"What happened?" I asked in a voice that didn't sound like my own.

"Don't you remember?"

"I remember a fire, and Ruben."

"Ruben set the house on fire and locked you inside. He nearly killed you."

"Where are we?" I asked as I glanced around the room. It looked slightly familiar but I knew that it wasn't our house.

"The house burned down, we weren't able to save it. This is Ben and Ellie's room."

I tried to keep my eyes open but they drifted shut again. It was very difficult to stay awake. All I wanted to do was sleep. I was exhausted.

<<<><><>>>

(PETER)

"Everything will be alright," He said when Ellie walked in the room. In her hands she held a cup of soup. Peter could see the heat rising up from it.

"Did she wake up?"

"For a minute or two then she drifted back to sleep."

"Did she talk?" Ellie asked setting the soup down on the small table that was next to the bed.

"She was confused. She doesn't remember everything."

"Just give her some time," Ellie said as she smiled down at Lydia. "She will be alright, she is strong."

"When does Ben want to start building?" Peter asked.

"Oh, he's already started," She replied with a look of anger. "I told him that if he has to do anything too difficult then he needs to ask someone for help."

"Because Ben is known for asking people for help," Peter replied with a laugh.

"Why don't you go out and help him? I'll sit with Lydia, I would love the opportunity to sit and put my feet up."

Peter looked at her suspiciously and she placed a hand against her flat stomach then motioned for him to move. He did as she asked and she dropped down into his chair and reached out to take Lydia's hand in hers.

"Come get me if anything changes," He said as he stretched his back after sitting down for so long. Ellie mumbled that she would and Peter reached for the door. "You know, if this one is a girl, you could name her Peterina."

"Good bye, Peter." Ellie said and he laughed as he closed the door behind him.

He made his way outside and walked over to where Ben had already started the construction of the house that would be Peter's. Ben's shirt was already wet with perspiration as he hammered in a nail.

"Did Ellie take over for you?" Ben asked as he straightened.

Peter nodded as he looked at the frame of the house. It was already taking shape. Peter looked at the door frame that was at the back of the house and smiled at the workmanship. Many of the men had joined together to work on the house. The men had first worked together to build Jack and Susan's house because they were going to be married soon. Then it was agreed that

Peter's house would be the second built. There were four men there other than Ben and Peter who were working. By the end of the day the frame would be finished and by the end of the next day the roof would be on just leaving them to work on the walls. If Peter closed his eyes he could see it finished already. Lydia could hang her curtains in the large windows. He could imagine the quilt covering their bed. Each of her little stitches holding it together.

He took a deep breath and picked up a hammer. "Yes, Ellie took over for me. I understand congratulations are in order?"

"She told you?"

Peter nodded.

"One day you'll have some of your own and we will be adding extra bedrooms onto this house of yours."

"I hope so," Peter said and smiled as he thought of his children playing in the shade of the trees that were growing in the yard. "I hope so," He whispered to himself as he placed a nail and hammered it into place.

Peter worked through the afternoon. He kept his hands busy and let his mind wander. After a few hours he heard Ellie call his name and he stood up wiping his hands on his pants. Ellie waved at him from the doorway of her house and he hurried over. She held the door for him as he walked in and went to the bedroom that Lydia was staying in.

Her eyes were open and she was sitting up. It looked like her hair had been brushed and she had on a clean night gown. It was clear that Ellie had helped her to get freshened up a bit.

"Hi" She said in a hoarse voice and tried to clear her throat. Peter wanted to reach out and take her hand but he was filthy from working all afternoon.

"How do you feel?" He asked and she gave him a weak smile.

"I feel very lucky, and I am sorry for what I said to you."

Peter ignored how filthy he was and he took her hand in his and knelt down at the side of the bed so she could look him in the eye.

"Everything is forgotten."

"What happened to Ruben?"

"He disappeared. He thought you were killed in the fire and he ran. He thinks that you are dead so there isn't any reason for him to come back," He said to comfort her and to convince himself. There wasn't any reason for Ruben to come back. And if he did come back then Peter would kill him. For now he could run like the coward that he was.

Lydia sighed in relief and winced from the pain in her ribs.

"You will feel much better in a few days," Ellie said from the corner. She walked forward and set yet another bowl of soup down on the small table next to the bed. "Perhaps you would like something to eat?" She asked and Peter picked up the spoon to help Lydia eat.

<<<><><>>>

(LYDIA)

Susan looked beautiful in her dress. Her dark hair cascaded down her back with the flowers that Thea had picked woven into it. She was absolutely perfect. Jack looked at her with wide eyes as she walked towards him. She walked arm in arm with her father Eric towards the man that she loved.

I glanced down at Peter's hand as it was intertwined with mine. I felt his eyes on my face and looked up and smiled at him. He gave my hand a reassuring squeeze and turned back to look at the wedding.

I looked around at all of the people who were sitting around me. Many of these people had become my friends in the short time that I had been in Chedix. They made the wedding special. I couldn't help but compare it to my own wedding with Peter. It had been a short informal event while this was beautiful and planned out. Delicious food had been made and people had traveled from other towns to witness the event.

Susan stopped in front of Jack and Eric placed her hand in his. She blushed and looked at the man who would be her husband in just a few minutes. Peter reached over to take my other hand so both of our hands rested in my lap. Her father went to stand in front of the couple because Susan had asked him to marry them.

Everyone around us went quiet as the wedding proceeded. Women dabbed at their eyes and children were quieted by a stern look from their fathers. I tried to listen to all of the words that they were saying to each other. Susan's quiet voice made it difficult to hear and Jack was a fairly quiet person anyway. Once they were finished making their vows to each other Eric took over the ceremony.

"Do you promise to love each other as long as you both shall live?" Eric asked the couple.

"I promise, as long as I shall live, to love you with all of my heart," Peter whispered in my ear causing a shiver to roll down my spine. I turned to look at him in surprise.

"And do you Susan, promise to love this man as long as you both shall live?

"I promise," I whispered to Peter.

"You may kiss your bride," Eric said.

Peter leaned down and pressed a kiss against my lips and the gathering around us cheered for the happy couple. I smiled against his lips and pulled away to stand up and cheer with the people around us. Jack had his arm around Susan holding her close against his side. She beamed at him and held onto his arm.

Peter wrapped his arm around my waist pulling me close to his side and I knew that I would stay there forever.